Best Spectral Wishes

Phil Budahn

Nelle, Nook & Randall

D1277639

by

PHIL BUDAHN

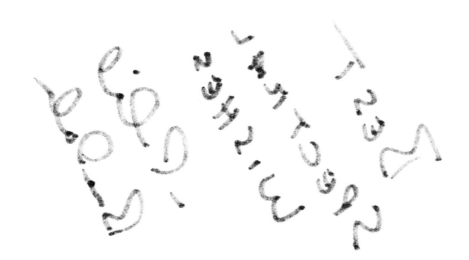

ISBN: 1492370339
ISBN 13: 9781492370338

CHAPTER

t started with fireflies. Flickering in a mayonnaise jar, sending beads of greenish-yellow light into the darkness. Gilda squatted on the porch of our duplex, her nose inches from the glass.

"They're avoiding each other," she said. "Each one's as far as he can get from everyone else."

I studied the blinking dots of light. "What do you expect? Fifteen or twenty born leaders in there, and not a single born follower?"

She shot me a look that died quicker than a firefly's spark. "I thought insects worked those things out. You know, queens and drones —"

"— hierarchies and lowerarchies," I added.

"— a place for everyone."

"Put yourself behind their antennas," I said. "If you were a firefly, who would you pick to follow? Every wanna-be leader in there would keep you awake with the light flashing from his backside."

The greenish-yellow glow of the fireflies sank into Gilda's black leather jacket without a trace. Nor did they have the briefest glimmer on her cheeks or metal chains, although bright specks ricocheted from the leaves of the honeysuckle below the porch.

"What do you think would happen if I put my hand in the jar?" she asked. "Will I get all itchy and woozy? Will I start dissolving into nothingness?"

"More likely, the fireflies will find a way to get out," I said.

She lifted a hand, her purple fingernails brushed the jar's glossy surface, and the fireflies darted to the bottom of the container and formed a swirling, twinkling, lime-yellow bundle. No concerns now in insect world about who was in charge.

"Hey," I said. "They can see you."

"So, will they attack me if I push my hand inside?" Gilda's eyes gleamed, her fingers thrummed near the jar. "Will they fry my vital essence with the power of their lights? Will I be blasted into more pieces of ectoplasm than can ever be reassembled? Will my being go twirling into the bottomless abyss?"

Nothing like an introspective specter, I thought, to take the fun out of an evening.

"One way to find out," I said. "Stick your arm in there."

Okay, maybe I wasn't making a serious suggestion. Maybe I didn't think central Virginia's most devoutly Gothic spook would stoop to do anything on my say-so. Or maybe I should have remembered that somewhere beneath Gilda's eyeliner and mascara a couple truckloads of indignation balanced on a hair-trigger.

"You'd let me do that, wouldn't you?" Her eyes bored into me. "You'd actually stand there and say nothing while I plunged my fingers into a jar of light."

"We're talking fireflies," I protested. "There's not a single healthy photon coming from the bunch of them."

Gilda's eyes gave off a black heat. "Some mentor you are," she said and left in a righteous *poof*.

Welcome to another night in the hereafter.

If having a heartbeat was such a good idea, you wouldn't be on the dark side of the daisies now, Cal likes to say.

I've always suspected there was a flaw in his logic, but whenever I try to pry it out, I get a headache.

Besides, it doesn't matter whether the advice makes sense. Cal is my sponsor in the 12-step recovery program of Specters Anonymous. He gets to run my afterlife. He also can tell me to stop talking, sit up straight and quit fidgeting.

I, on the other hand, don't get to tell anyone anything. Especially not myself. And in the rare eventuality that some night the seas would part, flotillas of flying carpets would land at JFK International Airport and Cal would let me serve as some other spook's sponsor, I will neither volunteer for, nor accept under duress, nor find a suitable bribe to take responsibility for Gilda.

One train wreck in my afterlife is enough. Thank you, very much. I'm my own accident-in-progress.

On this particular night, by the time I left the porch of our duplex a downpour began to pummel the empty streets of Richmond, punctuated by an occasional blast of lightning and a drumroll of thunder. My favorite meeting of the St. Sears group had already started when I floated through the basement door of an old church on the north side of Church Hill.

Gilda glared at me without actually looking in my direction, although an empty gray metal chair next to her began to exert a tidal pull. I gritted my teeth and, smiling at Mrs. Hannity and Darleen, nodding to Roger and Fast Eddie, wishing good evening to a few chairs that didn't, technically, have occupants at the moment, I struggled into a seat beside Hank.

He leaned over. "Gilda is putty in your hands. Everyone here can see that."

Hank has a *cafe au lait* complexion, a pigtail at the back of his head and more residual testosterone than anyone knows what to do with beyond the Great Divide.

I gazed about the room; most of the regulars were here, plus a sprinkling of newcomers. The newbies were easy to pick out: they were the ones actually listening to Fast Eddie talk about the swarm of killer bees that once descended on a city cemetery at the decisive moment to permit the escape of a couple hundred poor souls trapped in a stranger's tomb.

Among the details Fast Eddie edited out of his yarn (details being an impediment to the narrative flow) were the facts that only eight spooks had been trapped; killer bees were nowhere in sight, although reliable reports said flying coffee beans plagued one of the bad guys; and the coffee beans weren't airborne because of a deity but through Fast Eddie's secret skill at levitation, which would launch him out of our recovery group if Rosetta ever found out.

My attention snapped back online as Fast Eddie concluded, "And that's my story, and I'm sticking to it."

"Thank you for sharing your *perplexities, tremors and fantasies,*" said our leader, Rosetta, using one of the zippier phrases from our literature. "Who would like to share next?"

Gilda flicked a hand with purple fingernails barely poking beyond the cuff of her jacket. She usually let her black leather and chains do the talking for her.

"Gilda here. And I'm an old-fashioned specter," she said. "I like going to sleep before dawn and waking up at sunset. There are never too many shadows for me. Going down the street and being able to step right through people — I still can't figure out whether I want to puke or feel like I've died and gone to heaven."

Hearing one of the *H* words, Rosetta straightened on her chair. If it were anyone except Gilda, I'd expect Rosetta to get fussy about inappropriate language. Since our recovery program accepts members from all spectral persuasions, we don't want to be unwelcoming to the occasional atheist, druid or Zoroastrian.

Gilda had already broken her personal record for most consecutive syllables in a single evening, but she still hadn't picked the scab off whatever was bothering her. I suspected it might involve fireflies or wise-mouthed friends.

"Sometimes"— and here Gilda's eyes got a far-away expression, although that could have been her eyeliner undergoing a tectonic shift —"sometimes I wonder if I might look back some night and think that, maybe, I should let myself go. Become a rebel."

Most eyes in the room struggled to hold their focus. Gilda, our resident Goth, who drifted above the gray metal chair clad totally in black, except for the purple fingernail polish, the facial powder that glowed in the dim light and the bright red lipstick, thought she was too restrained?

Gilda lowered her voice. "I wonder if we should do more than talk to each other about what we think is going on. Maybe there's someone out there who knows, who has the answers. Maybe we should find her."

At that instant, a thunderclap rattled the foundations of Richmond, lights flickered, and when the illumination returned, one of the empty chairs in the back row had become a formerly empty chair.

The new arrival wore a three-piece suit, a fancy white shirt, and a tie barely wider than my thumb. His dark hair was slicked along the sides of his head and managed a peculiar wave-like construction at the top of his forehead. Wide and frozen was his smile, his eyes narrow and dead.

"Madame Leader, if I may?" he told Rosetta. "Brother Randall here. And I'm the dumbest specter on two planes of existence." Something close to a collective sigh rose from specters of a previously female disposition.

"I just happened to be passing by this wonderful meeting," he said. "I heard the heart-felt sharing that rose like incense from your devout members. And I wondered if I may be allowed to pass along an observation I once heard from a man far wiser than myself. Words that have meant so much to my recovery from the evils of sunshine."

Randall sopped up the attention like a dehydrated sponge. His squinty eyes probed the faces in the room. When that glance settled on me, I felt a cold wind. Brother Randall's look slid on to Hank and then to Mrs. Hannity. Only Cal kept his gaze level.

"That message is this —You're either digging your way out of your grave, or you're digging your way further into it. There's no status-quo here in the second life. We may be dead, but that doesn't allow us to lie around and do nothing."

Brother Randall's eyes rolled over the group again in triumph. Most of the spooks were leaning forward, their eyes gleaming. Except for Cal. Even Gilda stared with an expression I'd never seen before. Probably because it didn't involve granite stoicism or annoyance with me.

"I appreciate your kindness," Randall told the group. "And I look forward to hearing more about your recoveries from the terrible — and utterly false — temptations of living."

The narrow eyes that darted over the group kept darting and the smile that hadn't changed on Brother Randall's face continued not to change. Almost primly, he clasped his hands on his lap and slumped back on the metal chair.

The silence that usually settles on our meetings wasn't in evidence for the rest of the session. Newbies, who last night were fully preoccupied with looking cool and not drifting into each other, couldn't get recognized fast enough by Rosetta.

"Where have you been all my afterlife?" said one newcomer who was so far from figuring out how things worked in happily-ever-after that he had car keys hooked to a belt loop.

Half-time is an honored tradition for 12-step meetings on both sides of the Great Divide. For those of us with an aptitude for holding our breaths, there isn't much we can do except go outside for a couple minutes until the meeting resumes.

Hank had already drifted to the steps when I got there. The rain slanted through his spectral body; at any second, I expected to see droplets bouncing off the small ponytail at the back of his head.

"That spook sure knows how to raise the dead," Hank said.

"I don't know," was my best answer at the moment. I envied Brother Randall's confidence and vitality (*Note to self: Are we allowed* vitality *in the afterlife?*). But there was something about him that reminded me of the night I stepped in front of a searchlight and felt my ectoplasm getting blasted into cosmic dust.

"Did you notice the top of his head?" Hank continued. "Was that hair or a very shiny black helmet?

"Something about that spook," I started. "No, *everything* about that spook doesn't seem right."

Cal materialized on the edge of the sidewalk. "They're called *Spiritists*. Most of them want to sink deep roots into this second life. Burrow in, get comfy, give this existence 100 percent of all they've got. Even forget about our first lives or the breathers around us."

"Isn't that the point of recovery?" Hank asked.

Cal shook his head.

Realizing I hadn't jammed my foot into my mouth all evening, I joined in: "You've been telling us that we've got to quit thinking that we can return to the sunshine. Isn't that what Brother Randall is saying?"

"Randall wants to settle down here," Cal answered, "but I'm just passing through. I don't want to get comfortable. Some night, I hope to balance the books for whatever caused me to be sidetracked here. There'll be a *bing* and my sorry little attitude will reappear among a better class of spooks."

"We like you, too, Cal," I said.

Cal has never been accused of touchy-feely-ism. In fact, his theory of recovery tends toward the break-bricks-and-kick-butt school. But beneath that gruff, frosty exterior I knew was an interior that was gruff and merely chilled.

He and Hank went back to the meeting. I watched a line of lightning uncoil along the western sky, thought of Gilda's fireflies and wondered if she was really worried that a minuscule wattage produced by the bugs could endanger her transcendence. How could she possibly be frightened of fireflies? As I was heading back inside, I heard *clickety-clickety-clickety* on the slate footpath at the side of the old church and knew exactly what that meant.

Darting through the corner of the church, I tried to force my ectoplasmic heart to slow down. Petey couldn't possibly be here. The weather was terrible, home was a good ten minutes away, and she wasn't supposed to be out by herself.

As I emerged from the mortar and brick, I spotted an unmistakable package of fur, flailing tongue and eyes the color of hot chocolate.

"Petey," I cried. "What are you doing here, girl? You should be home."

Petey saw through my phony toughness and was about to go up on her hind legs to lick my face when she prudently slid to a halt and stood in the downpour; the beagle's tail worked back and forth with enough energy to topple her onto her side if she weren't careful.

I squatted and, cupping my hands around her shoulders proceeded to give the dog a good astral rubdown that went from her pudgy neck to the base of her expressive tail, all the while keeping my fingers a couple inches from the wet fur.

Dogs and cats can sense the presence of spooks in a vague, hit-or-miss way. Petey was remarkable for two reasons. First, she was able to see us directly. And second, she liked me.

Petey reacted to my astral cuddling as though it were the real deal. Guess I'll never know whether to put that down to some spiritual connection or a desire to please that ought to qualify Petey for another 12-step program.

"Let's get you out of the rain, sweetie," I said.

I glided to the base of the church wall, where overhanging eaves protected a narrow stretch of grass and pine needles. Petey shook out her fur, then settled on the ground. I drifted feet-first into the earth until my nose was nearly touching the beagle's.

"Now that that's taken care of," I told the wise, questioning eyes, "can you please tell me exactly what you're doing here?"

A bolt of lightning flashed, a thunderclap shook the ground, Petey shot to her feet.

"Easy, girl. I'm not going to let that big bad storm hurt you."

Petey had other ideas. She reared up on her hind legs and placed her front paws on the brick wall, and I realized I was about to see a beagle walk up the side of a building.

Or answer the call to the canine afterlife.

CHAPTER

etey is the finest, most perceptive and most dedicated friend on two planes of existence. I would do astral cartwheels to welcome her entry into the afterlife. But somehow, having a dog walk up a wall after it's sniffed its last fire hydrant seemed wrong. It was weird, it was unexpected, it was unbecoming. It was, in a word, feline.

The dog seemed to be in denial. She settled back on her haunches and stared at the roof.

"Only one way to be sure," I said, extending my hand toward her shoulder. Petey relaxed for another rubdown. My fingernail had barely passed into her shoulder when the beagle yelped and skittered away from me. *Have you lost your mind?* her accusing look said.

"Sorry," I said. "I had to be certain you hadn't become one of us. That is, one of me."

Petey snuffled, then turned her attention back to the roof.

"I hope it's not the Uber-Spirit calling you. Let me check it out."

Specters Anonymous teaches that we have to put our recoveries into the care of an Uber-Spirit. Although I haven't seen any animals in the hereafter, perhaps that's because the Uber-Spirit puts them in their own afterlife plane where they aren't reminded of the fickle dominance of men. Perhaps each species has its own Uber-Spirit.

It was time for the Uber-Spirit and me to have a reckoning.

Drifting up the wall and emerging through the roof, I was prepared for anything. But I hadn't anticipated that an all-powerful being who was concerned with the souls of mastodons and cockroaches might look like a large black plastic bag ensnared on the shingles, rippling and puffing in the wind. Or that it talked to itself.

Now, some of my fellow spooks might say a talking plastic bag is as reasonable an Uber-Spirit as anything else, and I'll confess that at the right moment, I might be a member of that group. But not tonight.

It wasn't the talking that made me a skeptic, but the fact that it was criticizing itself.

"What kind of an idiot can't remember where he put the nails?" the bag muttered. "How difficult is that? I mean, where could nails possibly hide on a roof? Or did some moron — and I'm not naming names here — forget to bring them?"

The lightning flashed, the thunder thundered, and I realized in a bloom of light that a man was using a black plastic garbage bag as a makeshift raincoat. A breather who moved a hammer a few inches, patted the outsides of his pockets and alternatively whispered prayers and mumbled reminders to have his head examined if he ever got off the roof alive.

He had misted-over, rimless glasses, a chin that reminded me of a chicken's, a receding hairline in which a patch of hair on top held its ground, and a tendency to recite the blessing before meals during moments of stress. He also had a name — Father Jenkins.

I've always been fond of the pastor: even though he didn't know about the 12-step meeting held every night in his church basement, I credit the priest's bumbling goodwill with setting the tone for our gatherings. Another priest might find a way to make the church less spook-friendly — perhaps by holding weekly classes for aspiring exorcists — so I wasn't going to wait for the storm to blow the pastor off the roof and send him squarely onto his cassock.

"Would you mind waiting here a moment," I told the unhearing priest.

Quicker than a gnat's cough, I zipped down to the ground. Petey had settled on the dry pine needles and was snoring. I headed back to the meeting. From the back of the room, I signaled Fast Eddie to follow me outside. Brother Randall watched the pantomime with his immoveable smile.

"This better be good," Fast Eddie said as we left the building. "The steam's building up in Brother Randall. I don't want to miss the big blow-up."

"What makes you think he's angry?"

"Them Spiritists came into our world pissed off, and they won't be happy until they've got everyone else riled up, too."

There was plenty about Brother Randall that made me uncomfortable, but Fast Eddie, was, as usual, taking things farther than the facts warranted.

"Interesting point," I said. "But I've got something else I need to talk to you about."

It was a simple problem: retrieve a small box of nails that were a couple feet below Father Jenkins on the roof, get them to a spot where he could find them, and do all this without letting the priest suspect that levitation was happening on sanctified shingles.

Of course, I hadn't anticipated the Goth factor.

"Oh, I can do that," Gilda said, materializing beside me on the roof. "Let me try."

"Try what?" I asked, delayingly.

"Levitating that little box."

"Levitate?" I looked at Fast Eddie and he wisely copied my expression of utter bafflement. "Levitate? Don't you know you'll never recover from mortality if you try to influence the physical world? You're supposed to be beyond mere materiality. *We have given up our old toyboxes*," I said, citing a passage from our literature that I find depressing.

Gilda glared at me through slitted eyes. "Perhaps you can explain, then, why it's okay for Fast Eddie to levitate those nails, but not for me. Hmmm?"

Because it's not good for either of you, I wanted to say, *but Fast Eddie already has a shaky recovery, so it won't do him much harm*. That zippy comeback, once unleashed, would shrink the small circle of spooks who will talk to me by two. Which wouldn't leave many more.

I bowed and backed away to give Gilda an open shot at the box of nails. "Be my guest."

Gilda slipped down the roof with an uneasy smile until the box was inches away. She stared at the container, she bit her lower lip, she glanced at me. The rain flailed the trees, the lightning begged for attention.

"Could you speed it up?" I checked the spot on my wrist where a watch once belonged. "I don't want to miss too much of the meeting."

For a moment, I could have sworn I saw rain sizzle when it came into contact with Gilda. But, of course, water and ectoplasm don't mix, and I was probably seeing the effects of a Goth straining the limits of her control over herself.

"This is just like the fireflies," she said. "You'd let me stick my neck out for a good laugh."

Gilda left with a wordless *poof*, and Fast Eddie soon had shingle nails crawling out of their soggy box, marching up the roof and forming three neat rows a few feet upslope of the padre.

Father Jenkins was so thrilled to find the nails that he didn't stop to wonder why he hadn't seen them earlier. After scooping up a half-dozen and stuffing them into his mouth, he worked a new shingle into a gap and hammered it into place.

"Whatever is the problem with our maintenance fund?" the priest muttered once he climbed down the ladder. "We've got to start taking water on the altar before anyone will move."

Once you involve yourself in a breather's problems, it can be tough to manage a graceful, ghostly exit. Still, if I had been able to answer Father Jenkins's question about the building fund, I could have changed some afterlives. Starting with my own.

By the time I got back to the meeting, Rosetta was in high outrage. Her enunciation was sharp enough to cut cheese, and her backbone — an artist's rendering of which is found in most dictionaries next to the phrase *no slouch* — was so straight it vibrated when she spoke.

"*Transcendence* means rising," she said. "And changing. Your idea of treating the here-after as your final destination goes against common sense, the basic principles of recovery, the English language and the traditions of this group."

In her look were surgically sharpened daggers that flew at Brother Randall, but his permanent smile never wavered, making me wonder if they can do colored tattoos on a spook's face.

"There are, as some say, many roads to the truth," Brother Randall calmly replied.

"That's *Duluth*," Rosetta snapped. "There are many roads to Duluth. But only one road to transcendence. And that involves working the principles of this program until we put this place behind us."

Brother Randall's shrug would take a semester of advanced psychology classes to explain. "I wish you luck with your experiment to bring hope to the still-suffering specter. As for me, I'm going to embrace this spiritual plane with the same enthusiasm I once embraced the physical world. I'm going to do everything I can to make the hereafter a destination of choice for my post-material brethren. I'm going to take the *dead* out of *dread*."

Mrs. Hannity raised her hand. "What are you going to do with the extra *R?*"

CHAPTER

"Robots, rutabagas, radar, recidivists." After the meeting, Mrs. Hannity took it upon herself to find a place in the English language for an extra R. She had the gusto; she wasn't going to let death keep her down.

"No, no, my dear," Rosetta said. "If you want a place for that extra R, you need a word that doesn't already have the letter."

Mrs. Hannity stroked her doubly-deathly white double chins.

"Let me see," she mused. "I always thought *jello* could use more letters. Something that gave it dignity. But that would leave us with *jellor*, maybe *jellower*, or even *jellro*. My, this is going to be more difficult than I thought."

Brother Randall couldn't get out of the room fast enough. Guess he was feeling guilty for setting an R loose on the world.

He drifted out the door, and as he hovered in the downpour, his eyes swept the splattered, glistening streets, the rain-darkened buildings, the street lamps standing in thin puddles of brightness. He was surprisingly average in height, Brother Randall was, but his head was out of proportion to the rest of his body. I believe he had enough material on his shoulders to provide another spook and perhaps a small teenager with something to decorate the ends of their necks.

Gilda watched me with a narrow-eyed squint.

"I'm sure Mrs. Hannity is the perfect person to find a place for another *R*," I said.

Truth be told, I knew I was going to pay for not letting Gilda try her luck with levitating those nails on the roof, a suspicion confirmed when she floated away from me with a flounce.

"You wouldn't happen to be jealous of him?" she said, glancing over her shoulder.

"Why would I be jealous?"

"Because spooks actually look up to him. Because they know they can trust him."

"They can look up to me, too."

A tweak here, a tug there, and I could stretch out my ectoplasm until my ears were fluttering in the jet stream. Then everyone would look up to me. But I knew that if I tried, Gilda wouldn't notice. Her interest was in Brother Randall, who was surrounded by newbies emerging from the meeting. Gilda joined them, although she was usually allergic to any collection of entities that could be called a group.

"What's your position on the Uber-Spirit," she asked Brother Randall.

"Everybody needs one."

"What if I can't find one that I can believe in?"

For the first time in our short acquaintance, the smile on Brother Randall's face actually changed. It grew larger.

"Then, until you do, I'll be your Uber-Spirit," he told her. "You can believe in me, can't you?"

Somewhere on this planet, on the two planes of existence that I'm personally familiar with, I'm sure there's a lawyer explaining to an irate consumer that she doesn't have grounds for a lawsuit, that a doctor is telling a patient she's fine and more tests would be a waste of money, that a car mechanic is informing a driver that the annoying rattle was just a loose screw and the mechanic wasn't going to charge a customer for fifteen seconds of work.

I'm willing to believe all those things that I've never seen, but I don't believe that I actually saw what happened next on the stoop on a rainy night after a meeting of the St. Sears group.

Gilda shot me a glance that was beyond the simply cryptic. She beamed at Brother Randall, stuck out her hand and said, "I like that. You've got yourself a believer."

"I don't believe it," I told Hank as we headed home at a breather's pace to accommodate Petey. "I simply don't believe it."

"You haven't burned off nearly enough hormones for the afterlife," Hank said. "I always knew Gilda was twenty miles of bad road. And then you come along, wanting to push the pedal to the floor on four bald tires."

"If I work at untangling that metaphor, will it be worth the effort?"

"Be like that," he said and *poofed* off.

The storm had ratcheted down by this time, and the rain was a fine mist blowing through the deserted streets.

Petey turned from the curb to flash a look of sympathy, then dipped her nose into the gutter and poked among the leaves, cast-off candy wrappers and fragments of newspapers that rushed in a swift stream to a grating at the end of the block.

Well, at least my dog understood me.

I let Petey set the tempo for our walk home. She kept trending uphill, with detours for any fire hydrant that had been visited by a fellow canine within the past week or any tree occupied by a squirrel within the month.

There was something calming in the red brick neighborhoods we wandered through, with rain dripping from the trees and the eaves overflowing and pattering to the ground and the cool breeze flowing from the swift heart of the river.

Staying in Richmond until the seas rose or another ice age shoved the gracious homes into the river seemed a nice way to spend a few centuries. After all, months ago, halfway through my first meeting of Specters Anonymous, I realized the group, for all its wisdom and practical advice, didn't have a clue what any of us were doing here. Gilda gave me my best hint one night when, writing on the fog, which was allowed during any month with an *E* in it, she showed me that the sign I saw as I was leaving my first life might not have said, *Exit*, but *Fix it*.

Then there was Hank. He had his own understanding of how the afterlife worked. He once said all spooks of a female persuasion would be here until they learned to whistle and the males until they lost the urge to spit.

That was as good an explanation as any.

Perhaps Hank could tell me why I had this empty feeling. Or why I was mumbling to myself that Brother Randall better be the best of all possible Uber-Spirits to Gilda or he was going to hear from me.

Petey and I reached the top of the hill where an obelisk lifted the statue of a Civil War soldier far into the starless sky. Petey picked up her waddle until she was almost scampering down a quiet, tree-lined, dead-end street to a duplex at the end of the block. A small shadow glided past the jar of fireflies on the porch. The beagle was moving so fast she nearly stumbled onto her own nose a few times.

The shadow on the porch, which went by the name of James William, jumped to the sidewalk.

"Petey girl!" James William said. "Where've you been? I've been awful worried. Mom said you might have wandered into the street and got —"

A sigh that would have moved the stoniest heart in the afterlife squeezed out of the boy's thin chest. He buried his head in Petey's plump, furry shoulder.

Petey looked over her other shoulder at me.

"You go ahead," I said. "I'll catch up with you later."

By the time I wandered back to the little park with the memorial obelisk, the clouds were scattering as though nature was embarrassed to have put on such an unseemly display before a city full of strangers, and the wind that added a graveyard's chill to the air had died down.

Gilda has gone to a Spiritist. It sounded like the chorus from an old blues song, something about spurned men riding the rails, train whistles echoing in the night, and small campfires set beside railroad trestles.

Next to Hank, Gilda was the spook I felt closest to. In a strictly non-icky sort of way. She had sought me out after her first 12-step meeting and even invited me to grab a bucket at Petey's house after a rogue Tosser (*translation: a spook who throws things*) had reduced the place I had been staying to kindling. Richmond hadn't been her first stop in hereafter, although she was guarded about where she'd been or why she left. "Portland" was as specific as she'd get about her last home.

Black leather and chains have never been part of my wardrobe, not even in ever-after. And I'm not sure that Gilda has ever sent much more than a couple dozen words in my direction on any given night. Yet having her go off with Brother Randall was a loss.

Which, come to think about it, was a peculiar way to look at the situation. I haven't lost Gilda. (A) she never belonged to me, and (B) she was just changing recovery programs. Criminy, you'd think she was traipsing down to the Hindu temple to thumb a ride back into the sunshine.

So why am I feeling like writing a blues song? Why's it suddenly so important to find a good rhyme for *engine*?

Above the river, three spooks whooped and careened beneath the clouds. Now veering towards one another and accelerating, now slowing down so abruptly they had to lean back on one leg although the maneuver threatened to topple them onto their backs.

"And this maiden, she lived with no other thought / Than to love and be loved by me."

This last observation came from the top of the obelisk. My old nemesis, Edgar Allan Poe, looked down as though drifting through a park was simply not done among the better sort of spectrals, while obelisk-sitting was quite the rage.

I fixed him with a glare that ought to tan his pasty little cheeks. "Do you really think you're qualified to give me advice about women?"

"Oh, well." Edgar A- studied his fingernails. "I was known as quite the rake in my day."

"Rake!? I'd picture you more as a shovel. For a honey bucket."

Poe jumped off the stone pillar and floated down. His eyes were wide, his cheeks puffed like a guppy's. "And you, sir, you dare call yourself a gentleman?"

"Not my best friends nor my worst enemies ever called me that."

The poet laureate of Richmond's dark side gave a crisp bow. "Then permit me to make that unanimous."

Poof-woof. Poe even dematerialized with a rhyme.

I'd started out on the wrong foot with Poe when I first arrived in the hereafter. And I've managed to put my worst foot forward ever since.

Maybe a spook with better transcendence would be more patient with him, more understanding or, at a bare minimum, not equipped with such a short fuse. I can't always say why he sets me off, but tonight, I had a moment of crystalline clarity into my own tangled motivations:

I absolutely refuse to take romantic advice from a man who was pushing forty when he married his thirteen-year-old cousin.

"You just tell me if I'm unreasonable to be a little touchy on that score. Huh?" I shouted at the top of the obelisk.

Was the stone soldier up there turning to give me an answer? Unfortunately, before I could investigate, I remembered another appointment.

I rematerialized in a section of Carytown where the trees consumed the front lawns of most homes and a generous share of the sidewalks. In the window of a brownstone mansion-turned-apartment-house, a flashing neon sign proclaimed *Psychic Advisor*, while a hand-written message on a paper taped below added:

> *By Appointment Only*
> *But not if you're desperate*
> *Or if you can't drop by later*
> *Or if you don't see a crowd outside*

A crowd? No. But I did see two spooks arguing near the stoop. I recognized Emily from a meeting I sometimes attend across the river in Marshalltown.

"You don't need to do it, Jake," Emily implored a spook who looked ready for the golf course. "You've got eight years of solid transcendence. Don't throw it away on a whim."

"But my Peggy is inside. I can't pass up the chance to talk to her."

"But does she want to talk to you, Jake? Does she need to talk? Think about it. Isn't it time for her to move on, too?"

"She can move all she wants. But I'm going to find out what she did with my golf clubs."

Jake pulled away from Emily, drifted up the concrete stairs and disappeared through the door.

"Hey, Emily," I said. "Rough night?"

"Happens every time the seasons change." Emily had the sweetest smile when she was exasperated. "The boys get anxious about their playthings. In another six months, they'll be staying up all day, worrying what happened to their deer rifles."

"For a spook to talk to a spouse, do you really think it hurts them? Or their families?"

"Anything that moves you to the fringes of the afterlife —"

"— moves you closer to the sunshine and a stumblie," I said, finishing one of the recovery program's many sayings.

(Note to self: How come we have 12 steps but 3,000 sayings? Shouldn't we call ourselves a 3,000-saying program instead of a 12-step program? Wouldn't that sound more impressive?)

With a wave, I drifted up the steps to the door of the brownstone.

"Hey," Emily called. "You're not going in there to take part in some voodoo ceremony, are you?"

"Depends on what you mean by *voodoo*," I answered.

CHAPTER

ime was when a psychic's office had over-stuffed armchairs, Tiffany lamps, tasseled velvet curtains, and wallpaper whose design was a personal favorite of Queen Victoria.

But Margie, formerly an aspiring actress and currently an aspiring psychic, let the pendulum swing too far in the other direction, past trendy, beyond with-it, landing squarely in a style that reminded me of a dentist's waiting room. As I drifted through a chrome frame chair with a molded orange seat and back, I saw *People* magazine, *Field & Stream* and *Redbook* on a side table. Should I have brushed my teeth earlier?

Margie and I go back. She is the only breather with genuine psychic ability I've met on this side of forever. We got acquainted while mutually pushing each other into — then pulling each other out of — a fracas that involved Edgar Allan Poe's first poem, plus a Tosser, and a tomb full of irritated spirits.

Ever since, Margie has been willing to help me research my past. I mean, my real past, the time when I liked the feel of the sun on my face, the sand between my toes and salt water squirting up my nostrils. Now with Gilda gone, I have all this extra time to find out who I was before most of me began turning into mulch.

Shouldn't I be thrilled?

Only two other entities were in the waiting room — the spook Jake whom I met outside, and a sunshiner with large hair and eye sockets tinted with the colors of a coral reef. She breathed, and I heard the faint, tortured squeals of seams struggling to keep it all together.

They'd been married. I could tell from the casual deliberation with which Jake ignored the woman and the smile on the woman's face that revealed the continuing celebration of a burden lifted.

I floated down a corridor to the back room where Margie met her clients. The last time I was here she was talking about chucking the crystal ball that psychics use to receive their visions. I wish now I'd taken the time to discuss alternatives with her; perhaps I could have convinced her not to replace the crystal ball with a goldfish bowl. Or, at a minimum, nudged her into transferring the fish into a glass of water when a paying customer was present.

"It's ecological," she said, glancing up from the fishbowl. She didn't have to be a psychic or a dentist to know what I was thinking.

"I'm relieved no one had to slaughter a herd of innocent crystals," I replied.

Margie stuck out her tongue.

A client who happened to be sitting on the other side of the fishbowl straightened. "Did I say something wrong?"

"No, I'm sorry," Margie answered. "I was reacting to a very rude spirit who just joined us."

"Is that the spirit of Clark Gable?"

"No, I think it's Bozo the Clown."

"Darn."

My turn to try traditional, non-verbal communication. I was unlimbering my face when — *thump, thump, thump* — a slow, steady series of vibrations came across the floors and walls, followed — *Woooooooooo* — by a low moan.

I clapped my hands like a bored theater critic. "Cheesy, Margie. Not very inventive. But I'll give you points for honoring tradition."

"Would you excuse me a minute?" Margie asked the customer. "I need to have a word with my familiar."

As Margie pulled herself to her feet, the client traced a finger along the sides of the fish bowl. "I'm beginning to feel that the little silver one with the wavy fins is trying to tell me something. Do you think that's possible?"

"The little silver one is quite gifted," Margie said. "If she decides she trusts you enough to communicate, you'll be very lucky."

The woman beamed. Nothing makes a person feel special quicker than being special to someone else. Even if that someone is a critter who likes dried flies and poops in its own drinking water.

I followed Margie down the hall to the back of the house. She had a small kitchen there, along with a slightly larger sitting room and a bedroom. Margie went straight to the sitting room and punched on the small television set and the DVD player.

I've wondered sometimes whether I might have been a psychologist in my first-life. How else to explain my awareness that Margie was distraught when the only clues were the three unsuccessful tries she made to place a DVD into the receiving tray on the player, and the fact that she only got it into the machine on the fourth try because of a lucky bounce?

"How's the psychic biz?" I hazarded.

"You people are killing me. Killing me. Does it make a difference whether I join you by suicide or starvation? Or do you insist on strangling the life out of me yourselves?"

"What do you mean?" I asked, hazardly.

"I don't have any customers. How can I run a business if I'm sitting in my room, alone, staring into my goldfish bowl?"

"But you have two customers now," I observed, more hazardly. "One in your consulting room and another one in your waiting room."

"This is their first and — I'll guarantee — last visit." She punched the play button on the machine hard enough to make the walls of the old house shake.

"And why is that?" I asked, most hazardly.

"Because you people keep chasing them away. Knocking on walls, making weird groans. It's so fake it's embarrassing."

"By *you people*, I take it you mean former sunshiners?"

"Don't you even dream about getting lawyerly with me."

An instinct for survival helped me stifle the observation that I thought she was responsible for the hokey, funhouse noises.

Margie stomped out of the room as the opening credits of a 1950s sitcom scrolled across the television screen. The title *The Honeymooners* appeared in grainy black and white.

During my inprocessing for the afterlife, I gave my name as Ralph, although I have no earthly reason why. Nor an unearthly reason. The name has always felt as awkward on me as four-inch heels and a bra. Leaving me to study the antics of an overweight, loud-mouthed, fictional bus driver in a sixty-year-old television sitcom for keys to my identity, all because he's the only entity I can think of who's also named Ralph.

Hank materialized above the sofa as the bare Kramden apartment appeared on the screen.

"I vote for vomit," Hank said.

"Are we talking about your lunch, breakfast or dinner?"

"For your name. Ralph, RALPH, *Ralph*. Doesn't that sound like some poor breather is hurling his guts out?"

"Ah," I riposted. "And where in my investigation does this clue lead me?"

"You got me there, Ralphie-boy."

I hate it when Hank does his Ed Norton imitation.

Thump, thump, thump. The panes of glass in the tiny window shook. *Wooooooooo.* A moan snaked through the old house. *CRASH.* The front door slammed shut. *CRASH.* And again.

Then the entire building shuddered as inanimate objects have learned to shudder when an irate human female walks down a corridor with a slow, there-will-be-blood swagger.

"Let's see what's going on here," I said.

"I'm with you," said Hank.

We set off to do our business, and only coincidentally, to avoid Margie, with a *poof, poof.*

As spectrals, we have the ability to be pretty much anywhere we want the instant we decide to be there. But even non-material entities have places they'd rather not rematerialize, my personal favorite being, from loathsome experience, an industrial-sized washing machine filled to the rim with soiled diapers.

With relative slowness, we worked our way through the floors and ceilings and walls directly above Margie's apartment, passing through pipes and electrical lines with no more trouble than wind zipping through a cloud.

The two floors above Margie's suite were used for storage. Floor-to-ceiling metal shelves snaked along the walls, leaving barely enough room for a breather to pass. Practically all the shelves carried cardboard boxes bulging with paper files and marked with the names of legal firms.

"Do you think," Hank asked as we threaded our way through the shelves, "that this might be the hereafter for paper? I mean, it's got to go somewhere."

"Kind of makes me wonder if the Uber-Spirit is running an archive."

In a small corner room on the third floor barely large enough for a respectable closet, the shelves were filled with hand-made pottery that only could come from a classroom of four-year-olds. Vases, tea sets, matching (in a mismatched sort of way) dinnerware, coffee mugs, beer steins, figurines, nativity scenes,

Easter bunny statues, and bas-relief wall-hangings featuring children with such large eyes that they had to be refugees from Area 51 — all brightly colored and professionally glazed, but showing the hand and eye of a single artist by virtue of certain features that they lacked in common, principally artistic design and surfaces that couldn't rip open an artery.

Hank would have whistled softly if he could whistle. "I think I've seen worse combat zones. But I can't remember where."

"Who has the more frightening mind?" I added. "The ones responsible for making this, or the ones responsible for saving this?"

"I vote for anyone who touched this garbage."

"I resent that."

Hank looked at me.

I shook my head. "I didn't say that."

"Of course, you didn't. *I* did."

The voice came from a shelf in the corner whose sole occupant was a purple ashtray. It had indentations to rest cigarettes on, sides that looked as though they'd been beaten by mice with boxing gloves, and a base that may have been left on a freeway for several hours.

CHAPTER

I floated until my nose was level with the rim of the garish ashtray. It was poorly designed, miserably constructed, and simply ugly.

"Are you in there?" I asked. Yeah, I know, I've got this gift for going right to the important question.

"Of course, we're in here," answered a voice, which for reasons of clarity, I'll identify as the Whiner. Coming from somewhere in, around or very near the ashtray, Whiner added, "Where else do you expect us to be?"

"Just want to be sure." I could have sprained an ear from listening so intently to get a fix on the voice's location. How difficult was it to find one tiny voice on a nearly bare shelf?

I was, as usual, ever the optimist.

For a second voice entered the discussion from the vicinity of the ashtray. "We have been waiting for you here, lo, these many eons." This voice I named immediately the Sniveler, who hastened to add, "And may I say that you cut an impressive figure. You were worth the wait."

"Thank you so much," I answered. "I hope I'm not bothering you. Just checking."

As best I could finally determine, the voices were spectral in nature and originated from the ashtray.

27

"You're just being thorough," Sniveler said.

"Speaking for myself," Whiner retorted, "I expected a little more, omni-science-wise, from a deity."

"What was that you said?" I asked. "The last word you said?"

"*Thorough*," said Sniveler.

"*Deity*," countered Whiner.

Hank struggled not to laugh. "They think we're gods."

"I was afraid of that."

"You know," Hank eyed me with unsettling interest, "I've always had my suspicions about you. You're so... so perfect."

"Will you cut that out?"

"We call him "— Hank raised his voice for the benefit of Whiner and Sniveler —"the Great God Ralph."

"We are not worthy, your Ralphness." Apparently, Whiner had decided that testiness wasn't going to get him anywhere.

"We are less than worthy," Sniveler added. "We are worthless. We are like as unto a boil on the backside of creation."

"That's going a bit far," I said.

"A pustule upon existence," Sniveler continued. "Whose every molecule is an oozing wart."

"Will you stop that?" I snapped.

"Yes, Deity," Sniveler sniveled.

A moan rose from the world's ugliest ashtray, a terrible, gut-wrenching sound, even for those of us without proper guts, a wail to shiver the ectoplasmic hairs on the back of my neck. Enough to make the wallpaper in the room wish it had someplace else to hang out. Is it possible for a spook to get a finger caught in a closing door? That was the first, last and middle thing that came to mind about whatever made such a noise.

Warily, I moved closer to the ashtray. "What's the matter?"

"We have offended our God." This was Whiner. "Ages and ages we have been lost in the darkness. The Deity, Ralph the Almighty, who has all of creation to worry about, finally deigns to take notice of us. And we insult Him. *Wooooooooo*."

Hank was rolling on the floor. He was also rolling through the floor, the shelves, the boxes of legal files, the walls.

Just when I start feeling good about myself, confident that I've learned where most of the levers and gears for recovery are located, something — or someone — plops in my lap that makes me feel like a newbie.

Once you start thinking you know all the answers, I remember Cal telling me, *you'd better look out. Because people are going to start expecting you to say something when they ask a question.*

I gotta have a long talk with Cal.

"Look," I told the ashtray. "You haven't offended me. I say unto thee, thou hath been righteous and faithful servants. Verily. And all I ask of thee is —"

"Tell us Lord." This was, I think, Whiner.

"— is that thou exitith thine container pronto. Forthwith and forsooth."

Perhaps you are acquainted with the silence that fills a crowded elevator when the riders realize that one of their number is responsible for a noxious bodily gas. The quiet that greeted my first commandment as a deity was about two and a half times quieter.

"What's the matter?" I finally asked.

"Well, sir, my lord." This was Whiner again. "That's something that I believe we've covered in our nightly prayers to you for a very long time."

"No, it's not," said Sniveler. "That's the only thing I've ever mentioned in my prayers. *Oh, god, whoever you are, whatever you may be, wherever you may be, please get me out of here. Pretty please, and thanks kindly.*"

Hank winked at me. "So much for quick fixes."

"Well, there is one fix I can manage." Turning back to the ashtray, I said, "I have been testing your faith. You both get an A-plus."

"Wowee," Whiner said, "A-plus and I still haven't finished my first hymn."

Sniveler popped up: "Wait till you see what I do with the cannon."

I favored Hank with a smug smile. "Impressive. They're already writing an official statement of beliefs?"

"No, I mean something to shoot non-believers with. You can't have a proper religion without punishing the infidels."

It is moments like that I'm sorry I can't sigh. Some idiocies can only be answered by sighs. I did my best with a puff.

"Listen unto me, my children. Here is my second commandment, which I order you to take unto thine hearts and use to guide your footsteps, from this day forward."

"Shoot," said Whiner.

"He just said he doesn't want us to do that," said Sniveler.

I put on my most regal expression. "I want no more moaning and no more knocking noises. That is all I ask of thee. Follow this commandment, and I shall answer thy prayers."

"Hmmm, I don't know how to bring this up, Almighty Spirit. But we've been complaining about the knocking for quite a while."

"It ain't coming from us," Sniveler said.

"What about the *Woooooo* part?" I asked.

"We are tormented by devils," Sniveler said. "They make me feel like I've been poured into a blender. Everything goes whirling. I have no control. I am sorely afraid."

"Ditto here, your Bossness," said Whiner.

"Stop it. I command it."

"If I may make a tiny suggestion, Almighty Godship." Whiner again. "Perhaps a little divine intervention would be in order to stop whatever makes us feel like we're getting pureed in a blender. Which is also the source of the howling that is not pleasing unto thee."

"That'd fix the old problemo in a tick," Sniveler agreed, in a groveling, oleaginous way.

"Let me mull this over."

Whiner was incredulous. "But aren't you all-knowing? What's to mull?"

"Think of this as another test," I shot back.

"I knew that's what it was," Sniveler was quick to add. "And a very fine touch, if I may say so myself, Your Immensity."

Hank and I dropped through the floors to return to Margie's sitting room, where perhaps the most decisive clue to my post-mortality had already whizzed past in an episode of *The Honeymooners*. Good ol' Margie would be more than happy to hit the replay button before she moved on to another customer.

The futility of that hope was soon revealed. For Margie was sitting on the sofa in her suite, with a boxed set of the television show in her lap, and the instant Hank and I reappeared, she snapped the box shut and tossed it under the TV table. The next instant, Hank was (*poof*) gone.

"Tell me something I want to hear," she said.

"You're not going to have that problem again."

Her lips said, "Oh," but there was *Naaah* in her eyes.

"Now that I've told you what you want to hear," I added, "let me mention that you may still have a problem."

"Pity. I also still have a DVD set of *The Honeymooners*. But that's only telling you what you want to hear."

"I don't like where this is going, but I have to ask: What don't I want to hear?"

"That I don't care if your nose falls off and your ears turn into sunflowers. You're not going to get me to touch another DVD so long as your friends are driving away my customers."

Specters Anonymous lets me spend time with fellow spirits who have glided further down the paths to transcendence than I have. Who swim in spiritual depths that I can only imagine. Who can teach me about detachment, serenity, and mastery of my emotions.

In fact, the instant I materialized in the diner, I could see my sponsor Cal demonstrate the full powers of his mastery of emotion. At a glance, I saw that Cal wanted to dismember Brother Randall, who hovered on the other side of the booth, but since Cal was advanced in the ways of transcendence, Cal just glowered at the table, his arms crossed over an astral chest as sturdy as a reinforced suit of armor.

"Of course," Brother Randall was saying, "that's just my observation. I certainly wouldn't dream of out-transcending you. Wouldn't dream of it, brother Cal."

"However —" Cal whispered.

"I can't help but wonder about your approach to recovery." Brother Randall glanced around the diner with a look that, had the breathers been able to see, would have started a stampede for the exits. "Why should we expect our spectrals to put aside the things of their first lives, when we surround them with reminders of their previous existence? Like this diner — with its food, sunshiners, beverages and temptations of the non-ectoplasmic."

"He means *flesh*," Rosetta whispered to Darleen.

Darleen shuddered while still managing to look confused.

"Well, even spooks have to be someplace," was Cal's quiet, clenched-teeth answer.

"Does that someplace have to have food?"

At this question, Gilda, who still wasn't noticing me, although this time she had a plausible alibi — a slice of French toast floating on top of a gallon of maple syrup that was left by some breather — shot upright. (*Note to self: Why can I sit up upright, but I can't lean down downright? If I lose balance and fall over, have I become downwrong? I sense in this conundrum a clue to my existence.*)

A half-dozen colors flickered across Gilda's face as she wavered on the verge of dissolving into a mist. She threw me a glance, and I swear I saw a beam of hardened titanium slip up her spine. Gilda hadn't become a Gothic member of the afterlife because of her sensitivity to other spook's opinions. Perhaps I'm the only one who can look beneath her glow-in-the-dark makeup and see signs of sensitivity. I knew that if Gilda had any disposition to being a Tosser, her next glance would have knocked the French toast to one of the outer planets.

"What's on your mind?"

Cal was looking squarely at me. Like the French toast, I thought this would be a good time to be elsewhere. But Cal wasn't my 12-step sponsor because he wanted to keep me happy.

"Speak, spook," he said.

"I was at Margie's. And, uh, one of her neighbors seems to have a couple spooks who have a problem. And I was wondering if we could talk about helping them."

"Wonderful," Brother Randall said. "Now, this is exactly what I was talking about. A spirit who is focused exclusively upon our plane of existence — helping other specters progress to fulfillment." Brother Randall downrighted himself in my downwrong direction. "Tell me, lad, what is the nature of their perplexity?"

"They're trapped in an ashtray."

"Pardon?"

"An ashtray. They got into an ashtray and they can't get out. They expect me to help them."

If Brother Randall were capable of being confused, I think I would have noticed it then. But Brother Randall was a Spiritist, a believer in the brotherhood and sisterhood of specters and a non-believer in mixing planes of existence. Confusion didn't enter into his view of the cosmos.

"Weren't we just talking about this?" Brother Randall asked Cal. "Weren't we?"

Cal stared back at the table.

Brother Randall zeroed in on me. "Spirits become involved in the physical world, acting as though they're still among the temporarily self-mobile. And what good comes of it? I ask you — What?"

"It's no big deal," I offered. "They seem to have found an Uber-Spirit."

CHAPTER Six

ometimes, my mind follows my mouth. I was on the verge of feeling sorry for Sniveler and Whiner because they thought they couldn't — or shouldn't — leave the vicinity of that ashtray, but they were happy, as I observed to no one's greater surprise than myself. Who am I to say Specters Anonymous is the only way to transcendence? Or to say they couldn't find spiritual growth in the world's ugliest ashtray?

Besides, this evening's meeting-after-the-meeting in the diner wasn't exactly an endorsement of the program. I'd never seen spooks so jittery about leaving someplace they didn't want to be. Suddenly, drifting through a reinforced steel door didn't look as easy as it once did. Would a departure soon after Brother Randall's mean they were siding with him? Would staying in the diner with Cal put them on his team? Where did the uncommitted, the uninvolved and the been-dead-too-long-to-care maneuver themselves in line to the exit?

Gilda practically ran up Brother Randall's back in her haste to keep up with her new mentor. I shook my head.

"Don't be too hard on the kid," Cal said. "Once the silent types realize they haven't been so silent after all, that all along they've been giving themselves miserable advice, they can be pretty quick to jump aboard the first bandwagon that rolls down the pike."

Cal and I were the last spooks to leave. There was no question where I stood. I tagged along when Cal headed toward Shockoe Slip. As soon as we rematerialized, Cal relaxed while he took in the cobblestone streets, the brick sidewalks in a herring-bone pattern, and the buildings dating to the 1800s.

"What if Brother Randall is right about recovery?" I asked. "Is there any chance we might be wrong?"

I didn't think answering *Yes* to one of those questions meant *No* to the other. Even in the afterlife, once we learn that sunshine can break down the essence of a spook beyond any hope of being put together again and that night is our constant, comforting companion, we still deal with shades of gray.

Cal stared at a break in the brickwork where a small tree had struggled up from the earth. He'd been some sort of mason or construction worker in his first life, and he found the old stones and bricks of this area endlessly fascinating.

While he studied the packed earth around that little tree, I took a closer look myself. There was only the tree, the metal cover over the exposed ground where it was rooted, the precisely tailored bricks that hugged the edges of that metal plate.

The sole oddity here was that one of the bricks was broken, and some passer-by had kicked loose a hand-sized fragment. I looked at the brick. I looked at Cal. I zeroed in on Cal's spectral fingers, which were clenched so tightly they were pink.

"Do you want to toss that brick?" I asked.

"More than anything in this world or the other one."

"Want to talk about it?"

"No."

"Of course not," I replied. "Why should you? Brother Randall didn't bother me, either."

Cal had been a Tosser during his early nights of post-mortality, one of the legions of spirits frustrated by knowing their first lives were behind them, that they'd already done (or not done) everything that they could in the sunshine. Tossers were basically bundles of rage careening across the astral plane who could manipulate small physical objects — rocks, silverware, plates, the occasional Chihuahua — and usually took out their frustrations against buildings, especially homes.

Once the brick has bitten you, I heard a recovering Tosser tell a meeting, *every time you look at your own hand, you wonder if it's good for anything else.*

We followed the street at a breather's pace for its downward curve to the lowlands of Shockoe Bottom, then looped back around to the old canal that paralleled the river. Cal had been an endless source of advice, companionship and directions that were clear-cut and straight-forward except when they were cryptic. But mostly, he was a way of connecting with something greater than myself or even the program of Specters Anonymous. I can't really say what that something was, but when I hear a spook talk in a meeting about a life force or spirit of the universe, I think they're getting close.

As we drifted along, I came to realize that Cal needed some of the advice he'd given me. *One night at a time*, or *Keep it spectral*, or *Don't pick up something if you don't know how you're going to set it down.*

That, however, would require me to open my mouth and say something, when a single glance at Cal's face was enough to cure a member of Yackers Anonymous.

We neared a spot by the canal and heard water rushing from an old lock; a freeway bridge overhead deepened the darkness.

I said, "Cal, I think we should talk about this."

Cal gave me the same look I got at our first meeting. I'd been checking out cemeteries in Richmond for headstones with my first name, hoping to find a last name chiseled into stone that sounded familiar.

That time he told me, "Follow me, kid."

This time he said, "Don't even think about it."

"Sure thing, Cal," is what I said on both occasions.

On the other side of the canal, underneath the overpass, was a sort of alcove, a nook, formed by the end of a pedestrian path and an earthen bank that supported the highway. Cal went there, and I followed.

In the thick shadows, I felt a sense of peace that only comes from places the sun never reaches.

"Psssst. Hey, buddy, you see any kids with flashlights coming?"

The voice came from the shadows high on the embankment.

Cal paused to study the darkness. "Do I look like the kind of spook who'd hang around someone who had a light?"

"Never hurts to ask," the voice replied.

I've seen specters who've squeezed themselves into crevices barely wide enough for a sheet of paper and I've met tomb-squatters who had the misfortune to find their actual gravesites and never left. Some of them have the consistency of smoke from the wick of a blown-out candle.

But I've never seen a spook who was completely invisible. That didn't make sense. If you've crossed the Great Divide, you're a spook, and if you're a spook, you're a real presence to your fellow specters.

Cal must have noticed my confusion. "Up by that drainage pipe." He nodded toward a concrete support under the highway. "A sort of darker smudge in the shadows."

"I see it." I started connecting dots. "Is that a real —"

"Yes," he answered. "That's a Shade."

"Your friend looks like he doesn't get out much," Shade told Cal.

"We try not to alarm the other spooks," Cal said.

"Heh-heh-heh-heh." Shade's laugh sounded like a small bird sneezing.

Shades are specters who are so terrified of sunlight that they attach themselves to one particular spot of darkness and never leave. You'll find them mostly in caves and warehouses. In time, they become flat, featureless and dark.

"You been here long?" Cal asked.

"Naw, I'm a newcomer. I wandered from the sunshine when they were building this canal."

Which would have been before the Civil War.

"You ever think about leaving?" Cal asked. "I know a good meeting nearby. Spooks with a few nights in recovery. I can guarantee you'll be home long before dawn."

"They're not interested in me," Shade said. "I'm no thicker than a louse's whiskers. They'll see right through me."

"That's a good one," I said. "*See right through you.*"

There's a first time for everything in the afterlife, and during the moments following that wisecrack, I was stared down for the first time by a smudge on the wall.

Eventually, Cal decided he was enjoying his chat with Shade and didn't want to keep me from getting together with Hank or Rosetta. His mention of Rosetta, with whom no one had ever had fun, told me Cal wanted to work on Shade. His failure to mention Gilda told me that he probably knew more about what was going on with her than I did.

Still, you never know where you'll find the next recruit for recovery. Until that moment, I hadn't realized you sometimes find them plastered to the walls underneath a bridge.

I went from the canal to my duplex on Libby Hill faster than a gnat can hiccup. Now, when I call it *my duplex*, I'm not using a sense of ownership that's based on the namby-pamby technicalities of the material world. The real owner, so far as I can tell, is the beagle named Petey, who has a small pet named James William, who has, in turn, a mother and a father of the breather disposition.

On this particular night, I drifted into the foyer, heard the distinctive *clickety-clickety-clickety* approach of Petey's toenails on the hardwood floor and squatted down to give the little fur bundle a good astral rubdown.

Petey came around the corner from the living room, looked me over as though measuring me for a dog collar, then clicked her way back into the interior of the house.

Even dogs are entitled to a bad night.

From the room where Petey disappeared came a voice that set my transcendence on edge and awakened the nastiness that used to live inside my head before I had the good fortune to die.

"No, no, no," the voice said. "The fault was all mine. When you said you knew a safe place to spend the day, I thought you were talking about someplace dark, where I wouldn't be disturbed. I assumed — and it certainly isn't your fault for being unable to read my mind — that you were talking about a place free of any infestation of Glow Bugs."

I zipped through the wall into the dining room in time to watch the final spasm of fake sincerity crease Brother Randall's brow. Gilda, I thought, was about to swallow her lower lip. She caught my eye, and when I mouthed the phrase *Glow Bugs*, she answered me with a glare that would have stopped a beating heart. Fortunately, mine only goes *rub-a-dub-dub* when I shake it.

If the hereafter's most zealous Goth, who won't stoop to admit that her funeral has anything to do with her lack of interest in getting a good tan, is made uneasy by Brother Randall, does that mean I'm supposed to make her feel better?

Besides, why in the Roth would anyone let themselves be dead if that meant they couldn't perk up a grim situation?

"By Glow Bugs," I told Brother Randall, "you must mean those little pests who are partial to certain hair products popular in the leading mortuaries."

Lest I be accused of subtlety, I gave the elaborately styled and heavily laminated curls on Brother Randall's head a close inspection.

Gilda shifted a little closer to the Spiritist. No question whose side that spook was on.

"Glow Bugs are what my friends call the sunshine-seekers who waste their time and resources on such, such —" Brother Randall was struggling to control himself "— such animals." He indicated Petey with a flip of his hand that no beagle deserved.

Hooking my arm around Brother Randall's elbow, I began guiding him toward the foyer. "I will give my colleague here a stern talking to for having exposed you to such an unacceptable condition."

I gestured grandly toward a window. "My, my, will you look at that? Where has the night gone? You must be on your way. Can't have a fine specter like yourself run the risk of being caught outside after sunup."

Brother Randall didn't budge from his place in the dining room, although I didn't notice that until I was horizontal in mid-air and Brother Randall shook loose my arm.

"It's too late to be outside." Brother Randall turned to Gilda. "I'm sorry. I must, after all, take you up on your offer of lodging."

"I'm sorry about that, too," I said.

For reasons beyond explanation, Brother Randall seemed to have decided to take no notice of my existence. I was, in a phrase, dead to him.

Gilda darted across the collection of antique coffee pots on shelves in the dining room where a specter could count on darkness during the daylight hours and no chance of being disturbed until twilight. She pointed out a nicely inlaid, early English pot, then another, a model taken from a design NASA carried to the space station, an art deco container that reminded me of a pipe-fitter's nightmare, and a pot that could have been an enlarged version of something from a little girl's tea set.

"And let's not overlook this little gem," I added, indicating the antique where I had parked my ectoplasm for many nights. "A multi-purpose friend for breathers called to the open road. In one handy, one-handled container, you have a shaving basin, drinking glass, cooking pot, knickknack container and, when the musical inclination takes you, a tin drum."

"Very nice," Brother Randall said. He studied the collection of coffee pots lining the shelves. His eyes swung back to me as he asked, "And which is your — I believe the phrase is — bucket?"

I nodded abashedly at that battered antique in the dark corner. "Some of us just can't relax around extravagance."

Brother Randall smiled. He bowed to Gilda, said, "I share that sentiment myself," then zipped into the coffee pot where I'd been sleeping.

Seven
CHAPTER

The place where a spook spends his daylight hours — commonly called one's *bucket* because ectoplasm gets pretty runny after staying in motion for more than fourteen hours — is a highly personal choice. And Brother Randall made a personal choice that duplicated my personal choice, which made things personal.

"Why don't you treat him with some respect?" Gilda hissed at me.

"Because his kind gives spooks a bad name."

"Noooo." Gilda stretched the word into four syllables. "Weren't you listening? Have you ever heard such a clear-cut guide to the afterlife, so practical and yet so transcendent?"

You used to think I was a pretty good guide I was about to say, but for once my speak-first-and-think-later method failed me. My name may be on a headstone somewhere, yet I was stunned to realize I still had things to lose.

Gilda gave me a glance that could have convinced a tomb-squatter to take a hike. "Brother Randall is different from anyone I've ever met. He's so firm, so insightful —"

"— so full of himself," I offered.

Gilda went from dreamy to deadly with a single *clink* of a chain-covered sleeve. "If you lay so much as a shadow on that specter, you'll regret it."

"Oh, and you'll do what to me?" I wished I still had heels to rock on.

"I'll make sure your bucket — with you inside — finds its way into a furnace before you can say, *boo.*"

Fire is nothing but sunshine blasting out from a pile of wood or a gas jet. A spook who winds up in a furnace can kiss this afterlife good-bye. Along with any other version of forever that might come along.

"That's not funny, Gilda."

"I know. I'm not joking."

That day, I can't pretend I slept much. I ended up in an art-deco pot with a spout that started at one end and couldn't find the other. Gilda had been a low-maintenance spook. Give that specter enough eyeliner, purple fingernail polish and pancake-batter makeup, and you'll think she spent her entire life dead. What had come over her now?

For a while, I heard Petey on the floor below the pot where I was spending the day. Every so often, she'd click across the floor and I sensed her staring up at the pot — my pot — that Brother Randall now occupied. Was she checking to see if I'd returned to the place I was supposed to be during daylight hours? Or was she protecting me from the strange specter who talked of spiritual growth but made me feel small the longer he talked?

I awoke as metal clanged on metal and my eyes filled with the dream-image of a dozen gas jets flicking at me with a cobra's hiss. Good thing I don't have adrenaline anymore, or it would have squirted from my ears by the time I flew from the coffee pot and into the living room. The light coming through the main window was gray and soothing, and I could see James William and Petey bounding down the front steps for their evening walk.

When I turned around, Gilda was behind me.

"I'm moving out," she said. "I thought you should know."

I looked down at her hands. Since it's tough to read a Goth's face, I've learned to read Gilda's fingers. When they're clenched tightly, she's feeling low. When they're clenched really tightly, she's okay.

Today, the fingers were unclenched.

"I'm bringing it up because I didn't expect you to notice that I've gone," she added.

I was still looking at her hands.

"See you around," she said and (*poof*) left.

Something you'll never find in the tourist brochures about the afterlife is that being dead is a group-project.

We're free to go our separate ways, although the loners I've met, like Shade last night or the occasional Tosser or the tomb-squatters at the cemetery, aren't ringing endorsements for rugged individualism.

Something about realizing you've burned your way through one life without anything to show for it tends to deflate the most rabid ego in the second life.

But I don't want to talk about Brother Randall.

After kicking around the old homestead for a while — watching Petey's mom in the kitchen assemble a beef stew without missing a single fanny wiggle as classic rock played from a boombox, browsing through the family's DVD collection to see if *The Honeymooners* was in the stack selected for viewing soon, and checking James William's room to see what's neat in case I'm suddenly reincarnated as a kid — I was lonely for some spectral companionship.

So, I did the old *Beam-Me-up-Scotty* trick that set me down inside the group's favorite diner in Shockoe Bottom by the old train station.

Roger, Rosetta, Darleen and some of the regulars were drifting around the stools by the cash register. The women would cozy up to any breather with an interesting dinner. Darleen was partial to mashed potatoes, and Rosetta usually held off committing herself until dessert, while Roger was content to sidle against anyone whose clothes had the stink of cigarette smoke.

I found Gilda alone in a booth in the back of the diner's half-floor, alone in the astral sense, although a couple of breathers managed to occupy most of the space on the benches.

She pretended not to notice me. If she had been staring at anything other than alfalfa sprouts on a plate, I might have been fooled.

"You're thinking you were a goat in your previous life?" I asked.

"I'm trying to lose my interest in food," she answered without looking up. "Going vegan is a good half-way measure."

"Does that mean no more drooling over rocky-road ice cream?"

Gilda gave me *that* look, the one that said it was still possible for me to end up in worse favor.

"Just answer one question," I said. "Then I'll go away quietly."

For a moment, alfalfa sprouts lost their allure, and Gilda actually looked into my eyes. She glanced away without saying a word, which for a Goth was better than a notarized statement of permission.

"Why are you so interested in Brother Randall? Can't you see he's as phony as a three-headed Siamese twin?"

"That's two questions."

"No, it's not. Not really."

The alfalfa must have started crawling away while I was talking because Gilda now couldn't tear her eyes from the plate with traces of arugula, goat cheese, dried cranberries and pine nuts that a breather, who needed this diet sixty-five pounds ago, was annoying with a fork.

"I want to get serious about being dead," Gilda finally said. "I want to get out of this place." She cupped a hand over her eyes, no doubt hopeful that anything she said wouldn't be traced back to her. "I need an Uber-Spirit."

"And Brother Randall can show you the way?"

"Brother Randall is the best I've seen here so far," she said softly. "When you stop playing the cynic, you'll see that's good enough."

I wanted to ask her what's suddenly so wrong with Cal or Rosetta, with whom she'd been spending time after some meetings. Or me. But I'd promised a short, no-hassle conversation, and we'd just had it.

I left as Gilda reached for a sprout. Her finger passed through the stem, which a spook's fingers will always do. Carefully, she pulled her hand back, made her forefinger and thumb into a pincer and moved cautiously forward.

I guess a believer is a cynic who'll give it one more try.

Back on the sidewalk, I hung around the area for awhile. The buzz of traffic on the overhead nearby sounded like surf rolling down a beach. A couple blocks away was the Edgar Allan Poe museum, where the old boy likes to hang out. It's safe for Edgar A-. He never actually lived there, which eliminates the chance of him being sucked into some sick post-life bondage to the place, and he gets to hear people who never met him say how swell he was, and women giggle and shudder when they talk about his ghost stories.

Yesterday, Poe was quoting *Annabel Lee* to me, and I wonder now if he saw my personal train wreck rolling down the track. *A wind blew out of a cloud by night / Chilling my Annabel Lee* came back to me from the doggerel I remembered from some grade-school. *Her high-born kinsmen came / And bore her away from me, / To shut her up in a sepulchre.*

Maybe dead men aren't allowed to have the chills, but the line about the sepulcher got me to stand up straight and quit fidgeting.

I was brought back to post-reality by a tap on my arm. (Specters, I should explain for those who haven't been paying attention, can experience something like physical contact with each other and with things that belong on the spiritual plane; exceptions to the rule are too complicated to go into now, seeing as how they involve phases of the moon, alignments between the North Pole and the Pole Star, and signs of the zodiac with a chicken.)

"Excuse me, sir, but could you be Mr. Poe, the famous poet?"

"I could be," I replied.

Could be, but wasn't a more scrupulous spook might have added.

The question came from a specter in a dress made of coarse fabric and a sun bonnet. Her eyes were a shade of blue that I haven't seen since my pre-croaker days.

"Oh," she oh-ed. And I wondered why I've been hanging around Gilda. Gilda couldn't pack so much movement into a single syllable if her afterlife depended on it. Now that I think about it, Gilda couldn't say *oh* even if she were reciting the alphabet.

"I have a few friends who are traveling with me," Miss Blue Eyes gushed. "They would be so honored — *honored* — if you could take a minute to greet them."

I let those turquoise eyes lead me a couple blocks down Main to the side of the Poe museum.

"Where are you from?" I asked.

"Cincinnati."

I rounded the corner and saw a hundred spooks lined up in three rows. To understand what I mean by *lined up*, imagine a set of bleachers occupied by spooks, hip-to-hip and shoulder-to-shoulder. Then erase the bleachers. That's what the crowd outside the Poe museum looked like.

My guide gave the group a smile so large the sheer weight of it bent her over at the waist. "Didn't I tell you he'd come?" she said. "Ladies and gentlemen, fellow Cincinnatians, it is my distinct honor — *honor* — to introduce to you the greatest American poet who formerly lived, Mr. Edmund Allan Poe."

So, names aren't her strong suite. The crowd went wild and, besides, I've never met anyone on any plane of existence who could move more while staying in one place than Miss Blue Eyes.

I tousled my hair, rumpled the front of my shirt and tried to make my eyes look haggard yet ethereal.

"My friends," I said. The cheers were enough to wake the living. Spooks jumped up and down, wept, clasped their hands to their bosoms, tried to get my attention by tearing strips of ectoplasm from their arms to wave, even went into spontaneous combustion.

"I'd like to share with you —" more applause "— excerpts from my greatest hits."

I'm glad I only promised excerpts. If I'd promised to recite an entire poem, I'm sure the cheering would still be going on.

I raised my arms, a hush fell over the group. My little guide managed to force her entire body to stand still.

I cleared my throat and let a poetic mistiness cloud my eyes and said, "The glory that was Greece, and the grandeur that was Rome."

They went bonkers, they did cartwheels, some lit out for the moon like Roman candles, some plunged into the bowels of the earth in paroxysms of ecstasy.

Again, I lifted my arms. An exhausted silence draped over the crowd. I intoned: "Helen, thy beauty is to me like those *dee-DUM-dee* barks of yore."

Grown spooks collapsed to the ground, specters stood with tears streaming down their faces, little children were bug-eyed and silent.

Without giving them a moment to collect themselves, I threw out the big one: "Quoth the raven, NEVERMORE."

The crowd lost all self-control.

$\mathcal{E}ight$

CHAPTER

CHAPTER

f I hadn't followed my excerpt from *The Raven* with something from *Three Blind Mice*, I think the performance might have had a stronger finish.

Still, the Cincinnatians were happy, my little blue-eyed guide was breathless (in a beguiling post-respiration sort of way), and I knew enough about myself to realize I was five seconds from seeing if my audience — they were from Ohio, after all — could be convinced that Edgar Allan Poe actually wrote the lyrics to *Ninety-Nine Bottles of Beer on theWall.*

So, I bowed, blew a kiss to Little Blue Eyes and, instead of walking around the corner with something resembling dignity or disappearing into places yet to be determined with a sudden *poof,* I zoomed into the sky like a sparkler, did a couple loop-the-loops over the museum — to, I must say, an encouraging chorus of *oo's* and *ah's* — and was over Norfolk before I realized my graceful exit was a hundred miles behind me. I turned around and slouched back home.

Halfway up the Peninsula, Richmond sparkled like a string of Christmas lights tossed onto a basement floor. I settled on top of the Confederate memorial that stood on a hill on the eastern edge of the city, barely a block from the duplex where I kept my bucket these nights, assuming, that is, that my bucket wasn't now Brother Randall's bucket.

Spooks in tattered gray uniforms were sprawled on the grounds around the pillar that was capped by an over-sized statue of a rebel soldier. Still infused with the sweet intoxication of poesy, I stood on the dark air next to that carved soldier and declaimed:

"Once upon a midnight dreary, while I pondered weak and weary —"

"— and my breath was getting beery" came from below.

Squint-eyed, I stood my ground — as it were — and continued:

"*dee-DUM, dee-DUM, dee-DUM* came a rapping as of someone gently tapping —-"

"— or of someone loudly napping," the guerrilla poet said.

I flung my arms wide and screamed, "*dee-DUM, dee-DUM* Quoth the raven —"

"— Get out of here!"

This last line was punctuated by a battered boot hurtling through the night, followed by a shower of boots, some with parts of legs still in residence.

Before I'd even become a proper artist, I had sipped the bitter vintage offered to every martyr for art. I left behind the slings and arrows and boots of outrageous literary criticism and decided to see if anyone had shown up early for the regular meeting.

The St. Sears group of Specters Anonymous derived part of its name from its original downtown location. The other part came from some of the group's founders who thought it unseemly to hold a meeting dedicated to such a noble purpose in a department store. So, in an example of savvy marketing, instead of changing locations, they added *St.* to the name and continued for decades in their original location until that site was converted from a department store into a rubble pile, which inspired the regulars to relocate to a church basement.

On my glide-path to the meeting, I noticed an unusual light inside the church and, finding no early arrivals in the basement, zipped through the ceiling to investigate.

A circular curtain had been set up to one side of the pulpit, ten or twelve feet high, surrounding a statue. Inside that strange cocoon, a bulb glowed, the only light in the dark cavernous building except for candles flickering near the altar. One person, maybe two, moved behind the curtain, and I heard the low murmur of voices.

Before I could poke my nose into clerical business, gliding up beside me like a ghost, was… well… a ghost. She had a veil over her head and looked doubtfully beyond her shoulder at the spooks scattered across the pews and choir loft.

"Excuse me," she said. "Can you direct me to heaven?"

"Afraid not," I answered. "But I can get you to a good 12-step meeting. It's not far."

"That's very nice of you to offer," she said. Her smile was painful to see and probably painful for her to make. "I had my heart set on heaven. I'll just wait over here with these other people."

She slid into a pew. I went closer to the curtain.

Inside was Father Jenkins, who'd survived his night repairing the roof in the storm. He was steadying a ladder for Simon, the church caretaker, who sometimes barged into our meetings but, being a normal breather, wasn't aware that he was making himself into a pest for a roomful of specters.

"Just wiping it off ain't getting rid of that stain, Father Bob," Simon said, looking at the priest.

"Then try the cleaning fluid," Father Jenkins replied.

Simon pulled a bottle hooked into his back pocket by its nozzle. Before I could get a good look at what Simon was doing to the statue's head, I was distracted by a rapid-fire series of *ahems* that came near my left elbow.

I looked down into the face of a kid who had more freckles than a centipede has toes.

"Where's heaven?" he asked. "I gotta get there. They're expecting me."

"Go out the front door," I said, "then right along the sidewalk. Cross three streets, go to the second brownstone on the left. Tell them Max sent you."

"Swell," the kid said and took off in a flash. However, owing to his unfamiliarity with the mechanics of the celestial plane, the kid was heading to Australia the last time I saw him.

Wherever he ended up, he'd be better off than here. Maybe the spooks down the block or the ones in Australia could give him better directions. I couldn't.

I poked my head through the curtain again. Simon was spraying cleaning fluid onto the face of a plaster angel and scrubbing away the tracks of tears.

"I don't know why you're going to all this bother," Simon says. "At my church, we'd just shout *Hallelujah* and *Praise the Lord* and call it a sign from the Almighty."

"Yeah." Father Jenkins sighed. "But we both know it was a sign from the parish board. They should have let us fix the roof five years ago. Let's not confuse the faithful. Can you rub a little harder, Simon?"

When I turned around, I nearly bumped noses with a specter who'd managed to smuggle a cigar stub into the hereafter.

"Buddy," he said. "You gotta get me to the Pearly Gates."

I shook my head. "I hate to be the one to break the news — but you're going to have to see the folks at the mosque for directions."

To get out of the church, I had to push my way through a horde of spooks desperate to find out what they should do next. By the time I made it to a door, I wasn't responsible for what I said. Fortunately, I think the most frequent answer I gave to the question of the moment — *How do I get to heaven?* — was *Be nice to your mother.*

It's not that I have a negative attitude toward religion, it's just that I think the clergy are pretty weak when it comes to follow through. I expected them to have enough clout with the folks in charge of the afterlife to have free booklets at the exit doors at the processing center for happily-ever-after or maybe a list of the top 10 things new arrivals need to know emblazoned hourly across the sky. What is so unreasonable about expecting some practical advice thumb-tacked on trees?

At least, by the time I made it down to the church basement, the guy with the cigar had decided to check out our meeting. I guess anything looked better than wandering into a mosque and asking whether it's too late to sign up for seventy-two virgins.

I brought him right up to the gray metal chair where Cal sat. I knew what was going to happen, but I kept trying.

Drop me into a meeting with my hair on fire, thirteen pint-sized demons latched to my arms and legs, and the first-edition of *Frommer's Guide to NeverNeverLand* clenched between my teeth, and Cal's first question is going to be — *What have you done for the poor, still-suffering spook?*

"Cal," I said. "I want you to meet a newbie I'm bringing to his first meeting."

Cal looked down at his knees. "Is that an introduction? Does your friend have a name?"

I looked at the newcomer. "What's your name?"

"Gwendolyn."

That got Cal to look up.

Gwendolyn shrugged. "It don't feel right to me, either. But that's what the last guy I saw said — this paper-shuffler behind a desk with a big book."

"If that's the case," Cal said, "we can call you Gwen or Lynn."

"Naw, I think I better stick to Gwendolyn. I don't want to get cross-ways with the big kahunas on my first night."

"Good move," I said and looked at Cal for validation.

Cal looked at his knees for entertainment.

Cal was being more Cal-like than I'd expect from Cal, especially within a thousand statute miles of a newbie. If Cal were a breather, I'd suspect he ate something funny for dinner.

I settled into place next to him, Gwendolyn on my other side, and heard a funny little voice come from Cal's seat. "This is my first meeting, too, Gwendolyn."

"Well, we're both in for an A-Number-One thrill," Gwendolyn said, unthrillingly.

Gwendolyn must have realized something strange was going on, for he took the cigar from his mouth, tucked it into his shirt pocket and studied Cal.

"Name's *Shade*," said the tiny, tinny voice in Cal's chair.

Gwendolyn stuck the cigar back into his own face. "Gwendolyn here. Nice seeing you there."

"Well, you gotta look fast," Shade answered with a chuckle.

That's when I saw him. Hanging underneath Cal's shirt collar was just the smallest sliver of darkness. Is it possible for a shadow the size of a squashed spot of dust to look *perky*? The dictionaries will have to redefine perky if they want to keep Shade from attaching the word to his inquisitive, two-dimensional self.

Moments later, other dimensions came into play as, through the door, emerged Brother Randall, the ever-smiling Spiritist, with a couple other regulars from the St. Sears group and Gilda — non-joining, uninvolved, doing-her-own-thing, semi-reclusive Gilda — following like baby ducks caught in the momma quacker's wake.

"I wonder if the group would indulge me." Brother Randall drifted along the edges of the room, while the others joined the circle of gray metal chairs. "I would like to lead tonight's meeting."

Rosetta had been the leader of this gathering long before Cal bullied me into my first meeting. Rosetta looked up, raised a finger —

And Brother Randall said, "Thank you, thank you. My friends, my family. I have great need of your solace and wisdom tonight."

Then, for the rest of the meeting, Brother Randall paced back and forth across the room and told us everything we were doing wrong — especially about how true transcendence demands a complete break with the things of our first lives. Getting together in a building erected and visited by breathers was just a tiny hover away from lying down on the beach with a bottle of suntan lotion.

"Dangerous beyond words, beyond reason, beyond your astral destinies. Dangerous, I tell you, to congregate in places favored by the lesser beings of the first life. What transcendent purpose is served by visiting such places as movie theaters, libraries and, most deadly of all, *restaurants?*"

He managed to pronounce *restaurants* in bold-faced-italics forty-six points larger than the font he was speaking in. Gilda shrunk from his gaze. Something told me she'd tried to squeeze her last alfalfa sprout in the diner.

"I've even heard," Brother Randall said, "and forgive me if I should lose consciousness by the sheer immensity of such madness — that some spooks have their buckets in the domiciles of breathers. That they actually plan and maintain and covet vile contact with the lesser orders who are unacquainted with the values of our noble dimension."

At that observation, most of the spooks in the room sank below the seats of their chairs.

I wish I could remember everything about our nightly existence that Brother Randall found fault with. Or, perhaps, to save everyone time, I should focus on the things that he liked. Or, at least, I'll focus on them as soon as one comes to mind.

When Brother Randall finally concluded and announced his sorrow that not enough time remained for anyone else to share their thoughts and feelings, I'm surprised my trousers didn't slide right off my spectral hips when I stood up.

I felt about six inches tall.

CHAPTER

thought I knew *glum*. Glum was a regular visitor at one time, not actually a friend, but familiar enough that if I passed it on the sidewalk, I'd mutter, "Good evening," and keep going without registering its presence. I thought I could speak thoughtfully about three dozen different kinds of glum and three hundred causes.

But let me tell you something: I didn't know glum. And nobody else can know glum until they've stood in the dark with a handful of spooks, not one of whom was capable of making a sound.

I'll tell you something else: the medicine hasn't been invented that can counteract the depressive effects of being around a handful of corpses who are having a bad night. Not being able to shake the memory of Gilda's glance as she drifted out the door didn't help my mood. Was she disappointed in me? Contemptuous? Or was I supposed to go hurtling off into the night after her?

The one time you can know with confidence that it's really not *about you*, Cal told me once after crossing swords with Rosetta, *is when you're convinced it's all about you.*

Finally, Gwendolyn looked around the group, his cigar butt bobbing up and down. "Geez, guys, you're acting like somebody died here."

"Well, technically, when you think if it —" Rosetta started.

Cal silenced her with a ripple of his eyebrows.

"So, this is what recovery is like," Gwendolyn resumed. "Very interesting, very insightful. I'd like to toss out an idea, if it's alright with you, about how you can make it better. That is, if you're open to an idea or two that didn't come from Brother Randall."

I summoned the energy to ask: "What would that be?"

"First, we find this hole. Nice and deep, but nothing highfalutin. Just your basic piece of ground that doesn't have any dirt for six or eight feet. Then, inside it, we cram the head of the guy who did all the talking tonight. Good thing his hair's already embalmed, huh? Then we top off the hole with the rest of him."

"Oh, we couldn't do that," Rosetta gasped.

But she had a twinkle in her eyes, and when she caught Cal's attention, they both put on matching grins. I looked at Hank, Hank looked at me. And I felt like a second-grader who'd just heard a poo-poo joke.

By the time we broke up, the mood was lighter.

"You know what would make this night absolutely perfect?" Cal asked.

"Finding a matchbook in this place that works," Gwendolyn replied.

"Nah," I said. "Only one thing on this side of the Great Divide can put a smile on Cal's face. And that is —"

"— *helping the poor, still-suffering specter*," Hank and I recited together.

It was one of the program's slogans, but Cal nodded sagely as though hearing it for the first time. "What a wonderful idea."

I don't need the obit page to tell me happily-ever-after is growing, and I didn't need Margie's magic fishbowl to guess what was coming next. So I reminded Cal about my strange encounter last night with spooks trapped in an ashtray at Margie's.

"Does that sound like someone who needs recovery?" I asked Cal.

Gwendolyn answered: "Sounds like somebody who needs a good kick in the astrals."

Hank gave Gwendolyn the squinty-eyed treatment. Hank has been the go-to-spook when something on this side of the Great Divide needs a little push, and he's always delivered with his own inimitable style. He wasn't used to some-one else providing the push and not worrying about style.

I flashed Hank my best insincere smile. Things were picking up on this side of the daisies.

So I led the delegation to the location of the newest — and best — psychic advisor in Richmond.

Margie was polishing her nails when we trooped into her parlor like an inspection team from the sanitation department. Margie barely registered our arrival.

"Did you come for the fire?" she asked.

I had no idea what she was talking about, but I didn't like it anyway.

"What fire?"

"The fire in the oil drum out back. Where I'm going to set a world's record for fastest incineration of five DVDs, called *The Honeymooners*. I think it would make a nice puddle. You boys want to place any bets?"

"I could use some of that action," Hank replied.

"Let me think about it," Gwendolyn mused.

"I'm not a betting shadow," Shade said. "But I've been known to try my luck with bingo."

Margie looked at the dark smudge underneath Cal's shirt collar. "You're new in town, aren't you?"

"As a matter of fact —"

She turned her silver file toward me. "The South's biggest fraud, Madame Sophie, is packing them in tonight. There's a convention of atheists in town. Those people will believe anything so long as it's not part of a religion."

"You still hearing funny noises?" I asked.

"The neighborhood watch is beginning to complain," she said.

"Let me see what we can do."

Margie turned back to buffing and polishing. "I'd suggest getting your marshmallows and weenies now."

Bending my knees, I got ready to zip through the ceilings and walls, but Cal restrained me with the slightest twitch of his head.

"Let's see what we've got here," he said.

He took us through a tour of the building, despite the fact that Hank and I had already checked the place out. I think Cal just wanted the chance to take a close look at something built by the hands of man.

I'll give Cal credit for thoroughness. He led us into the other half of the building. Anything within the exterior walls might account for the bumping and thumping that our two ashtray residents, Sniveler and Whiner, weren't responsible for.

Turns out, the side-trip was worthwhile. For the other front door outside led to a three-floor collection of nearly empty rooms, the sole exception being on the first floor, where, according to the fancy lettering on a glass door, Richmond's cheapest tanning salon was located.

The group of us floated in the dark hallway and stared at that glazed door like conventioneers outside a strip club.

"I... I... didn't know these places really existed," Shade said.

Hank's eyes were as big as saucers. "What's say we pop inside and give them a little *boo?*"

"Before the slip, comes the banana peel," Cal said. Not one of his catchier recovery sayings, but pretty clear.

Two floors up and on Margie's side of the building, we came upon the suite filled with legal files and, in a back room, an odd collection of mis-made pottery.

"Is anybody here?" I asked.

"Oh... It's him... Is my hair straight... Quit picking at that... *(Mumble, gurgle, glop)*."

This mini-chorus came from the off-center, off-line, off-putting purple ashtray on a shelf in the corner.

"All hail, the Great God Ralph." That was Whiner.

"Almighty, all powerful, all knowing, all everything." And Sniveler.

Cal threw up his hands, floated into the next room and, muttering all the while, "The Great God Ralph, the Great God Ralph," tried to bang his head against a box of legal files.

"It's not my fault," I shouted. "There's this misunderstanding."

"Oh, I was afraid of that happening," Whiner said. "We have presumed to know the mind of the Great God Ralph. We have sinned."

"Perhaps," Sniveler interjected, "if we have offended thee, oh godly one, you could make an example of the malefactor. And he will sin no more."

"Wait a minute." Whiner was showing some grit. "That isn't fair."

"Fair has nothing to do with divine justice," Sniveler countered.

"Nicely put," Gwendolyn said. He tapped the end of his unlit cigar against the ashtray. I could see Hank getting nervous. He didn't have any props to emphasize his ain't-taking-no-bunk-from-no-one attitude.

Sniveler and Whiner, meanwhile, went into a screaming fit. They *Woooo-ed*, they *Booooo-ed*, they curled the toenails of the gnats who were just trying to find an opening in the glass to get outside.

"Cut that out," I screamed.

One of the perks of divinity is being able to adjust the volume. It's like walking through the afterlife with a zapper that controlled everything.

I leaned toward the ashtray, my ten-cent mind trying to cash a twenty-dollar hunch. "You promised me that you were going to be quiet. Don't you know you share this... er... temple with another divinity? We call her Margie, and she is the goddess of —"

"Fingernails," Hank volunteered.

Alright, then. "Fingernails," I sighed.

"Ah," said Sniveler. "A goddess of fingernails. I didn't know such a being existed."

"Lucky for us, she didn't know you existed," Whiner snapped at his ashtray-mate. "Unlucky for us, she now knows we're here. And some spook — and I'm not going to name names — has made her sorely unhappy."

"But we tried so hard to obey, Oh Mighty Ralph." Sniveler was earning my reluctant respect: He didn't know the meaning of the phrase *piling it on too thick*. "We don't know anything about things bumping and knocking together. For the other stuff, we just lost all control. Our ectoplasm shakes when we want to be still. Our voices raise in wailing and whooping when we wish to be quiet from the deepest shadows of our beings."

"We couldn't help ourselves," Whiner said. "We were possessed."

I haven't put much faith in whiners or snivelers, in this plane of existence or in my earlier one, but those two spooks in the ashtray had sincerity. Put it down to the clear lack of cunning that it takes for a post-mortal entity to get stuck in the world's ugliest ashtray.

"Is that possible?" I asked.

"We're already spirits," Hank said, getting the jump on Gwendolyn. "So what could possess us? Used car salesmen? Insurance agents? Telephone marketers?"

Gwendolyn shuddered, and the ripples spent a long time working their way across his paunch. "Tupperware sellers. If I ever found one of them inside of me, I don't know what I'd do."

"Pull your head off?" Hank suggested.

With a yank, Gwendolyn reduced his own height by eight inches, which left the end of his neck looking for a purpose. Miraculously, the cigar butt was still clenched between his teeth, although his head was now in his hands near his waist.

"Naw," Gwendolyn said. "If there were Tupperware salesmen around, I don't think this would do me much good."

By this time, Cal had left the legal stacks and rejoined us in the room with the awful pottery and the ashtray with its own population.

"This spook," I pointed to Cal, largely for Gwendolyn's benefit, "this spook is one of that rare breed. A ghost whisperer. He can silence a banshee in mid-wail without raising his voice."

Gwendolyn drifted closer, still gripping his own head. "How does that work, boss?"

Acting as if he has conversations with headless spooks every night, Cal said, "First thing, you gotta lower your voice."

"Let me give it a shot," Gwendolyn replied. He set his head on the floor, then, never losing control of his cigar, said, "HEY, IN THERE! GET OUT OF THAT ASHTRAY!"

Perhaps I should have pointed out that being called *ghost whisperer* makes certain assumptions about loudness. *Don't waste your time trying to reason with someone who's already lost his head* is a piece of wisdom that never seemed truer than at that moment.

As Gwendolyn put his spectral head back on the end of his neck, I returned to the important question.

I said, "Why can't those spooks just hop out of the ashtray? I mean it's not that deep."

"I think I see a clue," Cal said.

"What?"

"It has to do with the color of their eyes."

I bent as close to the ashtray as I dared. If ugly could do damage, I was going to need a century or two to recover from that handmade wreckage.

"I don't see their eyes," I told Cal. "In fact, I don't see *them*."

"Bingo."

I hate it when Cal says that. Especially, when I'm still trying to figure out the question.

"Which means that —" I looked hopefully at Cal.

"Somebody's got to be upchucking his voice," Gwendolyn answered.

"Upchucking? Voice?"

"Yeah," Gwendolyn explained. "Like in *hurling*. Or *tossing up*."

"Hurling their voices?"

Hank leaned over to whisper: "Throwing. I think he means someone's throwing his voice. Like a ventriloquist."

I gave the ashtray a look every bit as ugly as it was.

"Is this some kind of joke," I asked it. "Are you really in that ashtray? I demand the strictest truth from thee, my somewhat loyal subjects."

"Can't rightly tell you where we are," Whiner said. "The decorations here leave everything to be desired."

"Describe them. The decorations, I mean."

"Well," Sniveler now, "I think as a creator, you've done wonders with this place. So open, so uncluttered, so begging for occupancy. Yet absolutely fascinating — innovative — for its use of voids."

"Can you see us?" Cal asked. Leave it to my sponsor to cut through the blue smoke to reveal the mirror.

Whiner replied: "Who said that? Another divinity? Another godhead whose head we haven't showered with godly praise. We are domed, domed."

"Will you cut that out," Whiner said, "And I told you before it was *doomed*."

"And what makes you so sure, Mr. High and Mighty, that it's not *domed*. I haven't seen my own fingers in so long, I think I'm growing hooves."

"I better check this out."

This last tinny remark came from Shade. He slid from Cal's collar and, like a flake of pure midnight cut from the sky, drifted into the world's ugliest ashtray.

CHAPTER Ten

By way of technical background, I should mention that I was recently involved in liberating six or eight spooks who were trapped in a mausoleum. *What's so peculiar,* I hear a scoffer scoff, *about spooks being in a tomb?* And why make a big deal about getting them out?

Spookdom is largely a rules-free zone. I mean, what's the point of having some entity wave a finger under your nose and tell you to look both ways when crossing a street when a column of Abrams tanks could roll through you without mussing your hair?

Being largely ruleless, of course, is not the same as having a blank rule book. One of the rules of this mostly anarchistic plane of existence — *Please take note: You may need to know this sooner than you think* — is that anyone who goes into another's grave, coffin, mausoleum or buried '65 Ford Mustang converted into a final resting place can't get out unless someone else — and I'm talking about sunshiners here — opens, uncovers, unlocks or rolls down the windows on the aforesaid corpse receptacle.

So when Shade slipped into an ashtray where two spooks were inexplicably trapped, every specter in that room wanted to snap off a smart salute and wipe away a tear. That poor, gutsy, misinformed little guy was putting his afterlife on the line.

The silence dragged on. Then it sprouted tendrils and hauled itself a little further. All of us were waiting for something along the lines of *Houston, we have a problem*, but nothing except silence came from the ashtray, and that shot up like water from a fire hose.

Sniveler had the lowest tolerance for calm.

"Hmmm?" he finally said. "Is there something we can do for you, Oh Magnificent Deity?"

"Do you see another spook in there? He looks like an ink stain, only thinner."

"Ink stain, ink stain. Can't say that rings a bell."

Finding a dark patch on a hideous, deep purple corruption of the potter's art wasn't easy, but I detected the barest suggestion of a shadow flowing from the center to the rim.

"Hey, Shade, do you see them?"

"I don't see anyone here," Shade said, tinnily.

Gwendolyn crouched until the end of his ever-chewed cigar brushed the rim of the ashtray. "If those jokers think they can pull my leg, they haven't seen my idea of hardy-har-har."

"Will you get that thing out of my face," Shade snapped. "I said I don't see them. But they're here. I can feel them."

When Shade emerged from the ashtray and returned to his spot underneath Cal's collar, we were a somber collection of specters. We needed to think about this conundrum. How can spooks hide from other spooks? And if it were possible, what else about the afterlife didn't we understand?

"I'll bet we wake up after a good day's sleep and the explanation will be right there under our noses," Gwendolyn said.

"But that'd mean we'd have to move our upper lips out of the way," Shade protested.

"We'll work that out when we have to," Cal said.

To fill the rest of the evening, Hank offered to show Gwendolyn the splendors of fraternity row. I was proud of my friend for taking the initiative in breaking any tension between him and the newcomer. Cal wanted to consult with some spooks with more post-mortality about the strange case of Whiner and Sniveler. And Shade, who hadn't been this far from the canal since the siege of Richmond, was anxious to get back home.

"I've had a really swell time," Shade said. "But sunrise must be, say, eight or nine hours away. I don't want to cut it too close."

Cal adjusted his collar over Shade. "Why don't you hitch a ride with Richmond's newest god, Ralph the Great. That is, if his holiness won't be offended by the presence of a mere specter."

"I can explain this whole deity thing, Cal," I said, cringing. I was beginning to sound like Whiner.

"Explain one thing." Cal looked at me with eyes that, for once, didn't find everything else in the room more interesting than I was. "Did you like it? I mean, being a god?"

"Well, it was different."

"Can I take that for a *Yes?*"

"'Natch."

So, I was assigned to carry Shade home, and this smudge-sized citizen of the Great Beyond wasn't happy with that arrangement, either.

Shade burrowed into a shirt pocket that I wasn't aware of having. That, in fact, I was certain I didn't have moments before.

"Eight or nine hours to get back to my nook," Shade prattled. "Let's round it down to seven hours. Then add a fudge factor in case we're tied up in traffic. That leaves us, at a bare minimum, four hours to get me back. Now, how long do you think it'll take. Don't sugar-coat your estimate. Just give me the cold hard facts."

"Have you ever seen a firefly blink?" I asked.

"Can't say that I have."

"Next time you're around one, pay attention. Because you'll be back home faster than a firefly can blink."

"What are you saying? That we don't have enough time? Oh, I was afraid of this happening."

Given my preferences, I would have headed back to my resting place in my antique coffee pot, in my nice, safe, Gilda-less home on Libby Hill. I could even spend some time rolling around the floor with Petey before the beagle and his family went to bed.

One of the things I like about happily-ever-after is that, if you find yourself with an appetite for drama, you can always zip over to the Globe Theater or Bollywood or Times Square or any theatrics department in any college in the world and gorge yourself on tragedy. We don't have to import drama into our own afterlives.

Speaking as a spook known for his disdain of the trivialities of the sunshine world, who is, frankly, becoming a legend throughout spookdom for his dedication to the loftier goals of the second life, I've sure stumbled into a blender.

At one extreme, there's knowing that as soon as Whiner and Sniveler figure out how to work matches, I'll be bathed in incense, joined by the adoration I saw in the eyes of dozens of spooks from Cincinnati.

On the other hand, there's Brother Randall's conviction that I — and the spooks who helped me the most in my afterlife — are doing such a rotten job with recovery that we'll all soon be sizzling on a grate at high noon in the middle of Broad Street, and Margie's determination that until the mess with Whiner and Sniveler is sorted out, I'm banned from *Honeymooner* shows on her DVD, which offer me the only hope of learning about my first life and moving on to the next plane of existence.

And somewhere on this fine night in Richmond, capital of V-A-, Edgar Allan Poe, who has me at the top of his personal list of foul smelling objects to avoid, is probably finding out that someone has been masquerading as him. No doubt, he'll put two and two together and come up with me.

And, then there's Gilda. The only reason I wasn't going to track down Brother Randall tonight and do something terrible, the nature of which I hope to figure out before I actually run into him, the only reason I was leaving him alone, was that Gilda is overdue for a break. Maybe Brother Randall had something for Gilda that she couldn't find in the St. Sears group.

A voyage of a thousand miles begins with a single step, Cal was fond of saying. *And a single step begins with moving your big toe.*

Don't you wonder how he finds the time to think of this stuff?

In my case, the big toe was muttering with the little toe about who should make the first move, and Shade was cowering in my shirt pocket, feverishly reworking the timeline necessary to get back to his nook in the wall by the canal before he's incinerated at sunrise.

I couldn't see how things could get much worse, short of getting trapped inside a mausoleum with Brother Randall, so I did another quick tour of Margie's storage room with its corner-to-corner, ceiling-to-floor metal shelves, and the little room crammed with a comprehensive collection of misshapen, poorly designed, miserably executed and stupidly colored pottery.

It was bad enough to pull Shade away from his computations for another glance at the ceramics from a nightmare.

"I had no idea," Shade said, "that the afterlife was this horrible."

"We ought to do a better job keeping out the riffraff."

I squeezed myself into the shelves and wove among the ceramics in a futile search for signatures. The artisan, who didn't have enough sense to stay away from wet clay and kilns, must have had legal advice that accounted for not implicating himself in so many crimes: there were no signatures on any of the pieces.

On the last shelf, in the back against the wall, I came upon a picture frame, lying face-down. I squeezed myself between the frame and the shelf. I was now not much bigger than the firefly's eyelash I'd advised Shade to study, and I zipped along the glass front and scanned an old newspaper article there.

Imagine reading *War and Peace* if each letter were the size of a twelve-story building. That was the sort of situation confronting super-mini-me at the moment. (*By the by, if you have the urge to read* War and Peace, *I strongly suggest putting if off until your afterlife. You'll be able to move quicker then, you'll have more time, and you'll be so up to your eyeballs in spooks that you won't feel bad about not remembering all those Russian names.*)

When I finished and returned to my paranormal size, Shade was clinging to the top of my pocket. "Don't you wish they executed the breather responsible for this garbage?" he asked.

"Not if it means that somewhere in happily-ever-after there's a lunatic sitting behind a pottery wheel."

"But why is anyone keeping this stuff?"

"The very point that interests me." I glanced into the shelves in the other room filled with neatly labeled boxes of legal files. "From that old newspaper article, I'm going to guess this stuff was made about fifty years ago by someone called Letitia Sanderling. And from the company that old Letitia's art is keeping, I'd also guess she got tangled in some legal problems."

I could feel Shade shaking thoughtfully. "That woman must have carried an awful grudge against clay."

CHAPTER Eleven

hade's dark little body trembled with the passage of each minute. "By my calculations, we have three hours and forty-seven minutes to get me home."

"Keep in mind that you've added a fudge factor of about five hours. And remember that we can get from here to there faster than a sparrow's hiccup."

"A sparrow's hiccup. You said earlier we'd be there quicker than a firefly's blink. Why are your estimates getting longer and longer?"

"Poor planning, I guess." I tried to give a reassuring smile to my blotchy fellow specter. "Before we hit the astral trail, I've got to give a quick report to the lady who lives here."

"That entity we talked to when we came in, that was a breather?"

"Yeah, some of them look like that."

I dropped through the floor and pulled myself together in Margie's consultation room, the one with the fishbowl and the ergonomic chairs.

I rematerialized practically under Hank's nose.

"I thought you were showing Gwendolyn the sights," I said.

"We were in the area —" Hank began.

Gwendolyn gave Margie a wink and added, "And there are some sights right here. If this little psychic wants me to leave, she can exercise me any time."

"It's not *exercise*," I snapped. "Oh, forget it."

Why was I bothered that Hank was visiting Margie? Do I harbor some sick attraction for a pre-croaker? Or was my vanity just perturbed by Hank's interest in Margie? And, if that was the case, shouldn't I revisit the second question?

Hank's abs didn't look so firm, his pig-tail so spritely.

"Later, spook," he said with a *poof*. Gwendolyn gave a shrug and (*poof*) left.

Margie pretended to be unaware of what was going on three feet away. She had a customer, a woman with hair the color of fresh snow and enough animal pelts on her body to stock a major trading post. That customer was accompanied by a middle-aged, slumped-shouldered male spook who managed to carry a henpecked, glassy-eyed appearance into the afterlife.

The woman sniffled into a lace handkerchief. Margie shot me a glance in which I could see burning DVDs. Shade floated down to the table.

"Hey, she's cute," Shade said, and any lingering doubt about the hormones that used to fill Shade's once-life-sized body disappeared.

"She has her nights," I answered.

Margie was determined to ignore me: I could practically hear her ears squeak as they closed shut.

With an impassioned sniffle, the woman said, "Can you, at least, tell me whether my Bernie is alive or dead?"

Bernie gave a double-thumbs-down.

"He's dead," Margie answered. "Most definitely."

"Is he here now?"

Bernie waved his hands in front of his face. Steam rose from his shoulders, which was pretty common for a new spook who's still working out the mechanics of dematerializing via the *Beam-Me-up-Scotty* mode of spectral transportation.

"He is." Margie fixed Bernie with the direct gaze that's unsettling when a spook receives it from a breather.

Bernie edged a few microns closer to the exit. Margie pursed her lips. Bernie decided to stick around.

"Can you tell me what happened to him?" the customer asked.

Margie's hands massaged their way around the fishbowl. She hadn't entirely abandoned the old hocus-pocus, despite her pride in bringing her profession closer to the twenty-first century.

"Bernie," she said. "Oh, Bernie. As a resident of the spiritual plane, you are beyond the petty concerns of our material life. You are a great spirit, a traveler among the mysteries of the universe. You are connected to the great recharging station of existence. Take pity on this poor confused woman, ah —"

"Iris. My name is Iris." Iris twiddled her fingers at a blank wall, hoping she was waving at Bernie, who was in the other direction and edging again toward the door.

"— Iris. Console her with the balm of understanding. Reach through the veil to answer her fervent plea. Tell us, noble spirit, how you came to unravel your mortal coil."

Bernie's mouth worked like a guppy's after a hard swim, but no words came out. Bernie seemed as surprised as anyone.

"You gotta give it a try, Bernie," I whispered. "You don't want Margie on your back for the rest of your second life."

Margie gave me a you-think-you're-so-smart look. Bernie's mouth puckered and pinched some more, this time adding a wiggle and a stretch.

"I think I see the problem here." Shade flipped off the table, flew to Bernie's face and darted into his mouth.

"What does he think he's doing?" Margie asked me.

"You'll have to ask him."

"If your friend messes this up for me, you'll wish you heard the last of me a long time ago."

Iris leaned over the fishbowl. "Why are you talking to my husband like that? I will not put up with anyone badgering my husband."

"Bernie has someone with him. A spook of the lower sort." Ol' Margie could be quick on the comeback. "I want that *creature* to leave him alone."

"It's a woman, isn't it? Don't try to protect me. I can take it."

A finger down Bernie's gullet should persuade him to cough up Shade, but before I could steel myself to the job, Bernie's mouth flew open and, glimmering in the dusky air, a fish took a smart half gainer between his teeth and landed in the fishbowl.

Interdimensional integrity was confused enough so that the fish wasn't visible to widow Iris (which was the way it should have been), but Iris saw the splash where fish and water met (which was a cosmic no-no).

With the coolness of one who is not surprised by unnatural wavelets in her diviner's bowl, Margie said, "Did Bernie own a boat?"

"No, but he liked to go fishing in the mountains."

"The veil is lifting," Margie said. "The nets, too."

Shade emerged from between Bernie's startled lips and, if a black smudge would give a big grin and wave, Shade was doing it.

Despite being a fragile little supernatural critter on his first night away from home in a hundred and fifty years, Shade decided that he'd like to hang around Margie's if I didn't mind.

Somehow knowing that Shade had residual hormones that Margie activated wasn't the same as knowing Hank had the hots for her. When Margie promised to tuck him away for the day in a rice pot on the top shelf of her kitchen; that sealed the deal.

"Don't think for a paranormal minute that I've forgotten you," Margie told me, waving a finger in front of my face. (*Note to self: Next time Cal asks me to update my thanks-a-bunch list of things I'm grateful for, remember to mention the rarity of women waggling their fingers at me.*)

Margie fixed on me a look that would make a lesser specter squirm. "Are you making any progress on getting rid of that hokey thumping and rattling that's driving away my customers? You better be."

"Or?"

"You're only dead, buster. Don't push your luck."

I left Margie's at a breather's pace. In the distance was Monument Avenue, where spooks came from across the country to see genteel homes from another era with porches and columns and magnolia trees in the front lawn. Nearby, at the intersection with Hamilton Street, behind beveled glass windows, the city's fraternities and sororities were cutting loose.

From time to time, a gray spark peeled off from the parade above the street and rocketed into the stratosphere. Fraternity row is popular with spooks from the Civil War: some Johnny Rebs can't figure out whether they're appalled by or envious of the modern notions of having a good time, and the sheer pressure of that indecision makes them pop off like Roman candles in tattered gray.

"My performance the other night, I understand, was quite satisfactory." Edgar Allan Poe was drifting beside me. His hands were clasped behind his back, his hair tousled, his eyes weighted with fatigue.

"In my day — in point of fact, in the days when I had days — I fancied myself rather successful with a quill," he continued. "But I must confess that I failed to appreciate the genius of my own compositional prowess."

Suddenly he was in front of me, a hand held to the breast of his black coat, the other stretched beseechingly as he declaimed:

"Helen, thy beauty is to me like those *dee-DUM-dee* barks of yore."

Edgar A- shook his rumpled hair. "Gracious, I understand now why I expired. I could never dare to write another line as pure, as elegant, as unambiguous as that. *Like those* dee-DUM-dee *barks of yore.* Come take me, Homer, Virgil, Milton, I am ready for the ages!"

"Let me explain."

Poe dropped his arms. "Do, please."

I saw in his glittering black eyes the fire that, in his time as a sunshiner, must have unnerved the female population of Richmond, New York and Boston.

"It was a homage. An act of respect," I stuttered, not sure what I was going to say until my ears found out. "Why, there's not a spook in all of Richmond that doesn't want to be you when he grows — er — moldy."

"An *homage.*" Poe gave the word a French do-over.

"I couldn't have said it better myself."

"Wanting to be like me, *n'est pas?*"

"All of us do." I was whimpering now. I wasn't happy where my mouth had taken me.

"Would you like to know who I would like to be? Or, better yet, would you like to see it?"

"Uh-huh," I answered, although I never felt less *uh-huh* in my afterlife.

"If I may trouble you, look behind. Just take the merest peek."

There was a bird back there. Its feathers were glossy black, its eyes glowed with the red of searing embers in a fire, its heart beat beneath its ebony chest with the controlled power of a speeding locomotive.

Definitely like a locomotive. Which was, roughly, the size of this animal.

This bird — a raven — towered over the porches and parked cars, the houses and trees. Over the fears of man and the dreams of specters. In its shadow, the night doubled up upon itself and the chill wind of a thousand cemeteries gathered.

"Do we believe our friend Ralph's explanation?" Edgar A- looked at the colossus in black feathers. "Do you, my friend, believe that Ralph was simply trying to honor me?"

Then Poe added, "Quoth the raven."

And the bird said, "Hell, no!"

CHAPTER

dgar A-'s attention wavered as the gigantic raven marched slowly toward us. A split second later, I was over the Atlantic and still accelerating. I hit my stride when the Dardanelles slipped below me, then coasted over the Indonesian archipelago. Somewhere around Easter Island I began to decelerate, although, unfortunately, it wasn't until I was approaching Kansas that I turned my thoughts to the near future. Specifically, to what I wanted to happen next.

Stumblies happen, Cal likes to say, *but recovery takes planning*. I always thought our first lives were about plans that had no relationship to what happened; therefore, our second lives would be about things that happened without planning.

Although I'm proud of that theory, I decided to give it a serious reappraisal when, one nano-second and one circuit of the planet later, I wound up exactly where I started from — between a black-eyed Edgar Allan Poe and a red-eyed raven the size of a building.

I needed a support-group urgently. With a *poof* to set me off, plus a spectral instinct that told me where the nearest concentration of spooks was and a *poof* to rematerialize, I found myself facing a flashing green neon sign. *All Problems Solved*, it said. At the moment, it was just what this specter ordered. I zipped through window of an old brownstone.

"Speak to us, Eloise. Raise your voice from the depths of the future and speak to us."

I was in Madame Sophie's parlor of psychic counseling. The lights were dim, the air was tinted with mystery and apricot brandy. Sophie sat at one end of a divan of brocades and tassels, while the other end was occupied by a youngish fellow with muddy boots, hair slicked *pro formally* across his bald spot and a dusty fedora in his lap.

A spook of the female influence shot across the room and grabbed my shirt. "Do you know how to shut this breather up?" she asked me. "I just want to let my grandson know that I'm okay."

Years of 12-step work helped me guess that she was Eloise.

"Some of Madame Sophie's microchips were put in backwards at the factory," I answered. "Your best chance is to keep things really simple."

Eloise crossed a Persian rug that must have been old when Alexander the Great was still learning how to pronounce Macedonia. She leaned into the paisley scarf that covered the hair and ears of Madame Sophie, once Richmond's most popular seer and biggest fraud, and now, since Margie's arrival in town, the undisputed holder of rights to the fraud title.

"OK," Eloise shouted into Madame Sophie's ear. "TELL HIM — OK."

"I see sand, vast stretches of sand, sand that would cover civilizations. I see cactuses and rattlesnakes. I see" — Why Soph didn't add a drumroll recording she could activate with her toe at moments like this was either a rare example of restraint or evidence of the old girl's declining mental powers — "I see… Oklahoma."

"No," Eloise screamed. "No, no, no. Do you hear me? NO. THAT'S *EN OH*."

"Wait. More information is coming." Soph was nothing if not adaptive. "It's *New Orleans. En Oh*. Your sister is living in New Orleans on Oklahoma Street. Or is it Oklahoma City on New Orleans Street?"

If spooks were capable of violence, Eloise's look alone would have made Sophie a goner.

"Isn't that wonderful," Sophie gushed at the grandson. "Your grandmother still has many years head of her. She is happy and cheery. If you could hear her laughter, as I do now, your slightest care for her well-being would drift away."

"You stupid old bat," Eloise said before stamping down her foot which, being a spectral foot uninfluenced by the material world, propelled her into the basement.

"And your grandma advises," Madame Sophie called out to the departing client, "to wear your hat. Richmond can be chilly this season."

Sophie, you must understand, was not without her powers. She's able to hear messages from the astral plane, only, it's as though…. I was going to suggest that it's as if Soph has wax in her ears and can't hear well. But that doesn't really state the problem. Imagine Madame Sophie's head encased in a block of wax, several feet thick. Position a brass band around her head, playing *St. Louis Woman*. Then try to talk to her in a normal voice. That'll give you an idea of the sort of reception Sophie gets from the ever-after.

Still, I'm in no hurry to write the old girl off.

"Letitia Sanderling," I said after the client left.

Sophie began to putter with a feather duster that rearranged the dust on the bric-a-brac that covered every table and shelf in her parlor, adding fresh wisps of feather with each swing to the debris already caked there.

"Letitia Sanderling," I repeated. It was the name I'd seen on the old, framed newspaper near the ashtray that had trapped Whiner and Sniveler.

Sophie worked her way through the knickknacks littering the corner shelf by the front wall.

Before I could repeat the name, through the window I saw Brother Randall drift grandly over the sidewalk, followed by a couple dozen specters, some regulars from the St. Sears group (most notably, Gilda), a few in-and-outers who passed through the 12-step program during their frequent trips to and from stumblies, and a fair number of newbies I suspect Brother Randall swept up at the cemeteries, the newspaper's obit desk and fraternity row.

Brother Randall was gesturing expansively. From a distance, he reminded me of a real estate agent showing off property to clients. For all I know, that could be exactly what he was doing.

Madame Sophie's soft, muttering voice drew my attention back inside. Sophie was on the divan with a figurine of a pretty little ballerina in her hands.

"You could have been big-time, Letitia. I told you I could almost see this little lady breathing. Once I'm sure I saw the wind rustle the hem of her skirt. You had magic, kid, not the kind I've been pretending to have all these years, but a magic of your own. The magic of the true artist."

"What happened?" I asked.

"As if anyone knew." Sophie waggled her finger at the figurine. *(Note to self: What's with all the finger wagging lately? Are women finally running out of words?)* "But I have a pretty good hunch, Letitia. You naughty little girl."

Sophie's conversation with the ceramic dancer grew animated, but any connection was lost between Sophie's misfiring synapses and Letitia Sanderling. Sophie turned to discussing roles she and the figurine had performed in their younger days.

From the bay window, there was no sign of Edgar Allan or his bird. Nor Brother Randall and his devotees.

Still, I wasn't going to take chances with an irate poet, a dead preacher or the future star of the motion picture, *The Bird that Ate Richmond*. I dematerialized in Sophie's parlor and pulled myself back together in Petey's home.

The house was dark and comfy, Petey must have tucked his family into bed. I couldn't tear my eyes from the New Age coffee pot that had been Gilda's recent bucket at sleep time. It had a spout and handles twisting in all sorts of directions, and it didn't take a psychic or a shrink to make a link between that ungainly pot and Gilda.

Beneath Gilda's gothic, I-don't-care-about-anyone-or-anything exterior was an interior where a little girl, dressed in laces and crinoline, just like Letitia Sanderling's porcelain ballerina, wanted to come out and play. A youngster frightened by thunder and needing a hug from time to time from mommy or daddy. Who needed something — and someone — to believe in.

Maybe that little girl was still somewhere. But if Gilda ever found her, she'd stomp the silly little creature into rat bait.

I dove into the battered, hobo-era pot that had become my bucket. Despite the residual smell of Brother Randall's pomade, I focused on the aroma of bad coffee that had just a *soupcon* of soap scum. Soon I was drowsy.

Clickety-clickety-clickety. Before I could liquefy, I heard a beagle tiptoe across the hardwood and tile floors and peeked out.

Petey was staring at my pot, and when she saw my head emerge from the snout, her tail starting whipping back and forth strongly enough to throw her spine out of alignment. I popped down and soon had Petey lying on the floor while I gave her the world's finest astral rubdown.

Sunup was a good hour away. I was prepared to spend at least fifty-nine minutes staring into Petey's warm, appreciative eyes and big old grin. But Petey is a four-legged lesson that once a beagle has us properly trained, she's going to come up with another surprise.

In this case, Petey rolled onto her legs *clickety-clicked* into the living room and returned with a box between her lips. Not just any box, but the DVD collection of *The Honeymooners*, which she laid down at my feet, beaming like all get-out, like it was Christmas morning and her kids were unwrapping the keys to a toy store.

"Do I look that blue?" I asked her. "Well, you've got the perfect remedy. If only one of us could lift a DVD into the player and punch the power button."

Petey stared hopefully at me, with only the tiniest cloud of confusion. She was a genius among animals, but she still had a way to go before she understood English.

For the moment, giving directions didn't matter.

"Good girl," I said. "A very good girl. Good dog."

CHAPTER Thirteen

ny night that starts with a welcome from a beagle is a good night. Besides, as I pulled myself away from Petey, I realized I'd had the most restful day in a long time inside the old coffee pot. Isn't there something bracing about waking up to the smell of coffee, your mind relaxed, and suddenly know you've solved a major problem even before your head has cleared enough to let you understand exactly what the problem was?

If I could just quit worrying about the possible uses that old pot had been put to, I think I might have tried whistling.

Seeing Gilda's empty pot on the other side of the shelf made my spirits dip. But only a little. Things were dropping into place. And at any moment, I was going to realize exactly what was being dropped, who was the dropper, and upon which droppee it would fall.

At this twilight hour, Petey was usually waiting by the front door for James William or Petey's dad to take her for the early evening exercise and potty break. Instead, the beagle lay on the floor beneath me, her chin in her paws, her eyes fixed on the pot Gilda used to occupy.

I didn't need Petey to tell me that pot was empty. But something else was going on.

"Did that nasty old Brother Randall come back while I was sleeping?" But, of course, when I heard my own words, spoken aloud, I recognized their absurdity.

A couple of orangutans were more likely than Brother Randall to stroll inside on a bright afternoon. He was still a croaker: his days in the sunshine were the shadow of a memory.

The thing is, I'm not sure Petey would agree.

I told Petey to have a good evening and not to wait up for me. I would have liked to take in one of the meetings-before-the-meeting, but I had a lead to check out first.

Most newspapers have a spook who's there because he likes bedeviling reporters and junior editors. Usually these spooks are former copy editors; they're always called Sparky.

I found him in the sports department at the *Richmond Times-Dispatch*. Even with hundreds of specters milling around the building, looking for clues about their first lives, which, in turn, would help lead them to whatever comes after ever-after, Sparky was easy to spot. First was the green eye-shades. Then there was his glow. In the modern era of computerized composition, editing and printing, the Sparkys of the astral plane spend more time than is healthy poking around bits, bites, CPUs, motherboards and microchips.

Cal says a newspaper spook in recovery has no more chance of developing good transcendence than the obstinate newbies who wander the streets with the lunchtime crowd until their ectoplasm becomes as brittle as old lace and one good wind distributes to each continent a smidgen of everything they might have become.

If Sparky was aware of this grim prognostication — and he seemed too sharp not to know — it only heightened his *joie de morte*.

"Just one sec," Sparky said, giving me my first wagging finger of the evening. He leaned over the shoulder of an editor to study a computer monitor with the ferocious concentration of a neurosurgeon.

"Will you look at that," Sparky said, throwing up his hands. "Don't you just want to rip your eyes out of your head?"

I looked at the computer screen: *Rogers Ends Padres' Skein*.

"When's the last time you used *skein* in a sober sentence?"

I opened my mouth.

"I thought so," Sparky shot back before I said a word. "Ain't these idjits heard of modern —" which he pronounced *MUD-urn* "— English?"

I was on the verge of making a hybridly-helpful observation (*Note to readers: A hybridly-helpful observation is an idea that's useful to one party in a conversation and garbage to everyone else.*) that perhaps it was all a typo, when Sparky dove into the editor's computer.

Seconds later, the screen flickered, the copy editor slapped his desk and muttered: "There it goes again," and when the monitor settled into its regular glow, the headline above the story had changed to: *Rogers Ends Padres' Skin.*

"I am not going to be dictated to by a handful of wires," the editor grumbled. *Clickety-clickety-clickety*, faster than Petey running to her dinner bowl, the editor pounded the keyboard. He paused, studied the strange keys at the top of his keyboard, hit three in rapid succession, then leaned back in his chair.

"You just try to ignore my override command, you microchip monster."

Every screen on the floor flickered before that editor's monitor said: *Rogers Ends Padres' Skan [Check spelling].*

"Sanchez, you need help grasping the finer points of baseball?" a voice thundered from the other side of the room. "Or is it written communication that troubles you?"

"Coming, boss," the editor said.

As a defeated sigh filled one little corner of the sports department, *Rogers Ends Padres' Streak* appeared on the computer screen of a copy editor who probably wondered if it were still possible to get a job in his father-in-law's hardware store.

Sparky rematerialized next to the editor, again with the cautionary finger, which he didn't lower until the editor muttered some very naughty words, hit a button on his keyboard and the skeinless headline went to the next stop on its voyage to the presses.

Sparky dusted his hands. "A spook can find a lot of satisfaction being a programming glitch. Now, what can I do for you, young fellow?"

"I was wondering if you could access the paper's records. Anything you might have on a Letitia Sanderling."

Sparky rubbed a hand over his pale, glowing chin. "My job doesn't give me much time for 12-step meetings. But I've heard steppers say it's not healthy for spooks to have much to do with breathers."

A fine example you are, I wanted to say. But as part of my journey in recovery, I've come to appreciate the importance of what our program literature calls *restraint of fist and spit.*

"Actually, this is a recovery thing," I said with misdirecting precision. "We've got a couple spooks who are being hurt by something this Letitia Sanderling did. We need to learn a little about the old girl to help them."

"You idjit."

"I beg your pardon. What's unreasonable about that?"

"Not you, the other idjit. The one over there"— he stabbed the air at a morass of people, desks, chattering printers, clicking keyboards and nosy spooks in the center of the newsroom —"who can't seem to remember that we justify the letters to the editor, but let the editorials run ragged."

As strongly as I wanted to remind him that a newspaper is a forum for community discussion and he shouldn't feel compelled to justify the letters people write, I kept my peace. My rare dabbling with silence also stemmed from my loss to recall any editorials that had *run ragged*. The *Times-Dispatch* always had fine writers, although I think someone needs to show them how an adverb can fit occasionally into a sentence.

"About Letitia Sanderling?" I asked, coming to see that Sparky had plenty of get-up-and-go, but a short supply of sit-there-and-listen.

"I'll give it a quick look-see. Whatever I run into will come out over there."

With a nod, he indicated a side of the newsroom with three dozen desks, two restrooms, four windows, a water fountain, a bulletin board with handwritten messages tacked to the cork surface, and a printer the size of an SUV.

By the time I got there, the printer was jabbering, and the single piece of paper that dropped into a plastic tray on the side of the machine was an old newspaper article dated nearly fifty years ago with the headline. "Letitia Sanderling, Ceramic Pioneer, Missing."

Hastily, I scanned the article before the machine spat out a copy of the weekly horoscopes for Capricorns, hiding all written traces of Letitia.

I had seen enough, though, to fire up the ectoplasm that I use these nights for gray cells. Waving good-bye to Sparky, who was too busy complaining about *some idjit's* mistreatment of the English language to notice me, I headed for the cool evening air.

A hunch told me that Shade probably didn't make an overdayer at Margie's. Leaving his waterside nook for the first time in a century and a half was probably adventure enough.

Twice I went along the old canal paralleling the James that in olden times allowed barges to avoid an impassable, rock-strewn stretch of river before I recognized the highway overpass, the shaded, moss-smelling canal and the drainage pipe where Shade had passed most of his second life.

"Afraid last night I'd left the stove on," Shade said when I peeked inside the drainage pipe he called home. "Cal got me back here."

"I can understand this place's appeal," I said and was startled to realize that I meant it. The traffic overhead sounded like waves on a shore, real water lapped through the shallow canal, the reflection on the culvert cooled the city's nighttime glow — it certainly made the old coffee pot where I spent my days seem like a poor choice.

I was tempted to ask if he could use a roommate because, now that Gilda had left the place on Libby Hill, I didn't have much of a reason to go back. Then, I remembered Petey. To see those warm brown eyes and happy smile turn my way, or hear the *clickety-clickety-clickety* of her toenails on the floor — those were about the happiest moments I'd spent this side of a headstone.

"You'll pardon my saying so," Shade began, "but you don't look like you're having a good night."

"I'm looking for one nice moment that doesn't come with a catch or a price tag or a bit of nastiness to balance the scales. Just one."

"Have you noticed that little spot in the side of the canal?" Shade asked. "It's to the left of that big rock, where some sort of weed or sapling is just beginning to rise out of the bank. The water pushes it, and pushes it some more, and just when you're sure the weed is going to get pulled out by its roots — wait a minute, it's coming, coming — There! The plant snaps back."

"You're saying it's a parable?"

"Nah, geometry never was my thing."

"Then what's your point?"

"That nice moment you were looking for. I think you just had it."

"Yeah, maybe." And when I looked at Shade, now resting on a cool concrete wall that was part of the overpass's support, I saw in his compact silhouette something that reminded me of long ears flapping in the wind.

"Do you know anything about ceramics?" I asked.

"Those are the comics they have in Syria?"

"Close enough. What do you say we find a diner where a bunch of spooks are talking about recovery and stumblies and transcendence?"

"Do they ever talk about chocolate?"

"Yeah, as a matter of fact, I think this is show-and-tell night."

CHAPTER

al was drifting back and forth in front of the diner in Shockoe Bottom when we arrived. In the ten or twelve hours since I last saw him, Cal had developed a tic that, every couple seconds, flicked his head to one side.

Soon a pattern emerged. Regardless of the direction he was heading, Cal always flipped his chin toward the same spot. Toward a network of overpasses looping around the eastern side of the business district. Headlights slashed through the darkness, occasionally streaking over the roof of the train station and an enormous, cemented-over parcel of land where the railroad companies used to have warehouses and repair shops and extra siding for the trains.

"Who's over there?" I asked.

"Randall and his people?"

"*His people?*"

"Yeah, I understand his brand of recovery has a certain"— Cal, who didn't waste his afterlife gabbing, was always concerned about finding the right word —"appeal."

Recovery isn't pretty, I remember him saying at a meeting. *Cleaning up after the likes of us never is.*

"You coming in?"

He looked at me, looked at the diner, looked back toward the railroad station, and I knew if I didn't leave now, he'd feel even worse for not being able to make up his mind.

Shade didn't utter a sound, but I felt him going back and forth across the bottom of my pocket, pacing like Cal.

I slipped into the diner. Hank, Rosetta, Darleen, Fast Eddie, Gwendolyn and some of the old familiar faces had found an empty table in the back by the kitchen. I tried not to be too obvious as I scanned the tables on the mini-floor to the right for Gilda.

Hank caught my eye and shook his head. I settled next to him above an empty chair.

"What's with Cal?" I asked. "He looks like he can't figure out whether he wants to come inside or leave."

Darleen clasped her fingers on the table top. "He's a good spook. He's just being torn apart by this Randall business."

"Only tearing that's needed here is with Randall," Hank said.

"Yeah," Gwendolyn added. "Who's this piece of high-and-mighty ectoplasm what thinks he's better than you nice spooks?"

"This *piece of ectoplasm* is a Spiritist with his own standards." Rosetta, as usual, managed to speak with quotation marks, underlinings and italics. "He thinks we are tainted by our contact with the material world. And Cal is too much of a good spook to dismiss him."

"You're saying Randall is getting to Cal," I said.

"*Getting to* is a clear description," Rosetta said. "*Ripping to smithereens* would be another one."

About that time a pair of coeds sauntered toward the restroom in the back. Their clothing was sufficiently gaudy to attract the comments of the spooks of the female persuasion at the end of our table, along with the attention of Hank and Gwendolyn, who both remembered more than was good for them about why there were genders.

Hank rose to follow the coeds. Darleen rose, too, and stood next to Hank, her nose two inches from his left ear. Her face was blank and her mouth pursed, but thunderclouds boiled in her eyes. I had no idea our resident optimist knew how to glower. Slowly, Hank lowered himself to his chair before Darleen could say a word.

Fast Eddie drifted across the table to study me. "Looks like someone just found out his sponsor pulls himself out of his bucket, one leg at a time every evening, just like the rest of us."

My sponsor, I wanted to inform him in a blast delivered at volume, didn't go around levitating material objects, as Fast Eddie does. Cal accepted that his physical remains were giving a headstone a reason for standing there: he wasn't interested in finding a way to put together another three score years and ten in the sunshine. Nor was he pretending, like Fast Eddie, that the material world didn't have any interest for him, except for occasional moments of high drama and low comedy.

"Cal is okay." I winced at the hollowness of my words. "I mean, he's got a good program of recovery. He helps a lot of spooks."

Fast Eddie took on a mock-thoughtful expression. "Yes, but does Cal know the only way to recovery? Could he help more spooks if he — just to pull an example out of the woodwork here — encouraged spooks to avoid hanging around diners because that appeals to their memories as breathers. And, as we know, you can't be a breather and a spook at the same time."

Fast Eddie had been getting under my transcendence for a while. When I realized the only response I could come up with was *Oh, yeah?* I decided it was time to keep my mouth shut.

Still, I could hear Shade whispering from my pocket: "Don't let him treat you like that. Stand up for old Cal. Does this spook think he's something special if he bad-mouths Cal when Cal isn't around?"

"Who says I'm not around?"

Cal drifted next to the table. His arms crossed over his chest, his eyes gave the table equal time with each of us, his smile that was so hard to define — part shy, part solid confidence — laid across his mouth.

This was the old Cal. With one peculiarity.

When you looked at him, you were mostly looking through him.

Schlesinger's Third Law on the Conservation of Ectoplasm in a Post-Mortal Dimension says each spook only has as much ectoplasm as he or she died with. Your stockpile of the big E can diminish many ways, but never increase. Although, like everything in the hereafter, there are enough exceptions, if we went into full details, to take up half the space in *Ralph's Death for Dummies*.

Sunshine burns up more ectoplasm than all other causes combined. What else is in the list of the top ten guarantees for a short afterlife?

Manmade photons — searchlights, spotlights, grow lights and high-intensity reading lights if you stick your nose right next to them — take second place. Manipulating physical objects is probably next in line, which explains the shortage of Tossers to diddle with property values. A variant involves using your own ecto-plasm to create objects in the astral plane. The Confederate vets wandering around Richmond like tourists with their muzzle-loaders are using some of their ecto-plasm to stay armed. The Big E, to continue with our list, wears away through simple longevity, as every spook on a vigil at his own grave finds out.

Then there's the doppelganger effect, a term derived from the marriage of *dope* and *gang*, as in the phrase *That dope needed a gang, so he made himself into one.* An illustration of this phenomenon was, in a manner of speaking, staring me in the face.

"How're you feeling, Cal?" I asked.

"Fine, fine. Never felt better." I think Cal was smiling, but, since expres-sions weren't part of his nature, I'm not sure what he was doing with his mouth. Maybe he wasn't, either.

The coeds came back from the restroom, and they walked through him without the slightest shudder. I took it as an insult that a spook of Cal's transcen-dental presence didn't drop their body temperatures a few degrees.

Instead, Cal was the one who winced. "Don't you think it's time we headed toward our meeting?"

There was a chorus of grumbling, but every spook at the table, plus a hand-ful sitting in the booths with breathers, trying to master the fine art of breaking away a couple molecules of a Reuben sandwich or a millionth of a drop of a pomegranate and mango shake, got their ectoplasm in motion.

We arrived in a group outside the room in the church basement that was home for the St. Sears meeting. Everyone except for Cal. He was drifting by the door when we got there and gave us a little wave.

"What's he doing there?" Cal asked.

Cal was also next to me, gaping at himself by the door. Cal-2 (the one by the door) turned away as though whatever was going on in the room was more important than seeing himself in a gaggle of arriving specters.

"Is this some kind of a joke?" Cal-1 (who was next to me) muttered. "Am I supposed to laugh?"

He sauntered toward himself in the door. Like John Wayne swaggering into the Alamo, Humphrey Bogart walking into Rick's Place, William Shatner con-fronting an alien life form on Alpha Centauri.

"Which one do we want to win?" Hank asked.

"My money's on our guy," Gwendolyn answered. His cigar bobbed as he spoke. "Now, which one is that?"

Cal-2 turned slightly in acknowledgement that he was somewhat interested in the spook bearing down on him, although Cal-2 still shot quick glances back inside the meeting room.

They were several feet apart.

"Oh, dear," Rosetta sighed.

"I'll take that bet," Fast Eddie said.

They were inches apart.

"Tell me what happens." Darleen covered her eyes.

"Omygawd," Hank said. "They turned into a giant cockroach."

Darleen squealed. Rosetta left in a *poof*. Fast Eddie sniggered. Gwendolyn grunted.

Hank said, "Only kidding."

Cal-1 bore down on his doppelganger, who, at the last instant, turned to confront him. The two met. Cal-1's momentum carried them through the door. And none of us could see what happened after that.

"Final bets, everyone, final bets," Fast Eddie said.

I crossed my fingers, hoping that Cal had come out on top, even though I wasn't sure what I wanted to happen or which Cal I was supporting.

I glided through the door, followed by my companions in recovery, only to find Cal floating in his usual spot above the gray metal chair facing the door. He was the only Cal in evidence and, unlike the wispy wraith who showed up in the diner, was as solid as a specter gets.

Randall and three or four dozen spooks were already in the room. I'd never seen such a turnout at a meeting of the St. Sears group. They were floating on the ceiling, stacked three high along the walls, poking their heads up through the tiled floor.

"Give us a couple minutes, will you?" Randall said. "We're almost at half-time. We'll be leaving then for the second half of our meeting."

"*Your meeting?*" Rosetta snapped. Rosetta was the chairspook of our meeting, and she protected it as though her afterlife depended on it.

Randall was as calm as an oil slick. "Yes, our meeting. The one that will follow the true principles of Specters Anonymous. That will break all unnecessary ties to — and contact with — the physical world."

As Randall spoke, I studied the faces of the spooks in the room. *Adoration* was the word that came to mind, and when I found it glowing from Gilda's face — barely recognizable now without the possum-eyed eyeliner, flour-paste makeup and fire-engine red lipstick — my stomach did a flip or two. Any notion I had about a happy happily-ever-after left for a long vacation.

"Is this really what you want?" I called to her across the crowd.

"Be still my silent heart," Gilda replied. "The great spook has stooped to notice me. We live in an age of miracles. Miracles!"

Randall raised his hands. "The issue before us is the creation of a new, true chapter of Specters Anonymous. With your grateful servant"— he pressed a hand to his chest and bowed —"as the chapter's leader. All those in favor, please signify by stating *Aye*."

A thunderclap of *Aye's* shook the foundation of the building. Security alarms went off in the church and in cars parked along the street.

"Thank you, friends, for your confidence," Randall said. "I am humbled and honored. This meeting is adjourned. To reconvene immediately with the rest of our fellowship at Libby Hill."

"*The rest of your fellowship?*" Hank said. "There's more?"

Gwendolyn raised a ham-sized fist that held his well-chewed cigar as daintily as a scalpel. "Hey, chief, what about asking for the *No's?*"

But Randall was busy. Busy chiding, shooing, pushing, urging and outright snarling at his followers to get up to Libby Hill or they could look for help from now on from the Glow Bugs and their patsies in the hereafter.

Gilda paused in front of me. I was about to say something, but a glimmer in her eye seemed to be daring me to open my mouth. On instinct, I kept my mouth shut because that was the opposite of what she wanted me to do.

Hey, who says dead men can't figure their way around.

The moment passed and she left with Cal.

Cal also stayed with us, sitting in his chair, the molded gray metal visible through his chest. His hands were clasped between his knees. Fear was in his eyes.

CHAPTER

ibby Hill overlooks the James River on the eastern side of the city. Below, the river widens and takes a hard right turn on its hundred-mile run to the Chesapeake Bay. On the eastern-most edge of the hill, where the slope plunges abruptly to the scrub wood and tall grass of the flood plain, is Petey's home.

Even though I knew Randall wasn't assembling his followers for an attack on my favorite beagle, I was nearly nuts with fear until I materialized in the dead-end street, saw the lamplight inside Petey's home, the blue flicker of a television, and the unhurried movements of Petey's family through the curtains of the house.

Hank was at my side. He didn't need explanations.

"Are we going inside?" he asked.

"Nah, I'm just a little jumpy." I pretended to know what a deep breath looked like. "When Randall said he was bringing his followers to Libby Hill, that didn't mean he's going to Petey's house."

The pigtail at the back of Hank's head looked steely with resolve. "Things aren't going to settle down here until Brother Randall gets his own planet."

I looked at Hank with renewed respect. I've always seen dignity in his little duck-tail, but now I noticed a healthy confidence in the black t-shirt that stretched across the tightest abs in two planes of existence, the slight glow of his hot chocolate ectoplasm. Did it matter if Margie and he were interested in exploring some inter-existential boundaries?

"When they made you," I said, "they threw away the mold."

"When they made me, they didn't use a mold. I walked straight out of the mountain."

We drifted down the block to the obelisk that dominated the hilltop, on the peak of which stood the statue of a Confederate soldier, rifle planted at his feet, his stone eyes fixed, not at the southern approach to the city, where battalions in blue once rolled forward in waves of cursing, sweaty, belligerent humanity. No, this statue's gaze was on Richmond itself. This was not a soldier on guard, but a farm boy in uniform staring wistfully at a place of enchantment.

Randall hovered in the air beside the obelisk. He glanced at the new arrivals from the St. Sears group with a sneer.

"I trust you had a good meeting," he said. "Final get-togethers should be memorable."

He laughed, and I heard thunder in his voice. His arms swept toward the horizon, from the river in the south to the tree-covered reaches in the east.

Other members of the St. Sears group drifted in. "Oh, my," Darleen said as she pointed downslope to the river.

Near the corner of the last refurbished tobacco warehouse now partitioned into loft apartments, high-priced restaurants and offices for software consultants, I saw a blur move slowly through the night.

Darleen and Rosetta bent their heads together and, with jabbing fingers, pointed out glowing blotches ranging from the base of the hill to the furthest reaches of vision.

"Spooks," Hank said. "An army of them. Heck, an ocean."

And like an ocean, they overlapped the banks of the river, flowed across the lowlands in astral tendrils growing into wider, fiercer currents that gathered strength and speed as they rushed toward us.

"Yes, my children," Randall howled. "Come to me. Come."

This was an ocean that obeyed the orders of a spectral lunatic, who wanted to stamp out the gentle wisdom of Specters Anonymous and replace it with his own shrill dogma for achieving transcendence. I began to feel uncomfortable.

A small, tinny voice sounded under my chin. "Does this sort of thing happen often?"

I had forgotten Shade. He pulled himself out of my shirt pocket and perched there, his little spectral chest pounding like a chipmunk's with remembered adrenaline.

"I've never seen anything like it," I said.

"Well, I have," Shade told me.

Hank and Gwendolyn joined the conversation.

"Like when?" Hank asked.

"In the war. I remember seeing thousands and thousands of soldiers in blue moving through those woods and along the river. Maybe from this very spot. There were more trees then, and that made it more frightening when you saw a patch of dark blue fabric coming through the shadows. Maybe the glare of a campfire on a brass button."

"You were a Reb!" Hank said. "I knew it."

"Don't hold it against me, because I don't think I was." Shade was thoughtful. "The only things I remember happened at night. I'm pretty sure my sunshine days were behind me then."

"So, what happened?" Gwendolyn asked.

"Well, we beat them off. Funny the problems that go away when you've got an army."

I shook my head. "Yeah, where are a few thousand armed men when you really need them?"

Hank punched the air, said, "Yes!" and darted into the night.

"This looks interesting," Gwendolyn allowed as he went after Hank.

Shade said, "Oh, Boy," and dove into my pocket.

I didn't need a Ph.D. — that's Posthumous Doctorate — for insight into the psyche of previous respirators, especially Shade. If I'd been on this hill before the fall of Richmond during the Civil War, watching armies maneuver on the plains below, the air saturated by fear, perhaps I'd end up spending a couple centuries in a nook under a highway, too. Why stick your neck out, even when there's not much that can be done to a neck on a non-material plane?

Closer and closer the mass of second-lifers drew, all the ragged glowing lines below converging on Libby Hill. Randall's cries reached a manic pitch. He was beyond mere words, his voice hurled primal screams into the dark.

The spooks on the hilltop had gathered in two clumps — at the foot of the obelisk near Randall's levitating form were his fellow Spiritists, including Gilda and Cal. Near the southern ridge line, where the view of the river was unobstructed and the ground sloped sharply downward, were Darleen, Rosetta, Fast Eddie and me. Plus the other Cal.

Gilda reminded me of the breathers in Father Jenkins's church, what with her intense concentration and the hands clasped at her chest. She had found what she wanted, an Uber-Spirit, and despite knowing Randall was a puffed-up jerk, part of me was envious.

Stillness descended upon the night. Not exactly like the crowd in a movie theater going quiet when the house-lights dim, nor even the silence that fills a church when the minister says, *Let us pray*. This was more like the quiet that comes when a fool shouting at the top of his voice from an obelisk takes a moment to clear his ears, and an army of spooks creeping toward him in the night stop for a moment to ask themselves where the noise went.

In fact, it was exactly that kind of quiet. And it shattered as thousands of ghostly voices filled the darkness with whoops and hollers, moans and screeches, and a few dozen noises that were beyond explanation. Voices twisted in a perverse tangle of anger, fear and jubilation.

None of the regulars from the St. Sears group could mask their discomfort in the presence of this madness. Even Gilda's eyes tightened in uncertainty. But Cal, the Cal who had left the meeting with Brother Randall, peered silently with leaden eyes and a cast-iron jaw at the spooks on the flood plain rushing toward us now at a fast clip.

I wasn't sure what the approaching army wanted. Knowing that Brother Randall approved of them was enough to move me in the opposite direction. The rest of my friends were reaching the same conclusion.

"Isn't this a good time to check out the hot fudge sundaes in Carytown?" Darleen asked.

A silly excuse, but more respectable than the justifications for leaving the area that were flitting between my ears.

Cal, my Cal, held up a hand. His eyes never left the plain, his face never registered the faintest emotion. I could see through him the other Cal by Randall at the obelisk. That Cal was on the verge of falling to his knees and salaaming his leader.

A *pop* came over my shoulder, from the direction of Petey's home. Another directly behind us, then a ragged volley that sounded like heavy stitches being ripped open by a seamstress.

Coming from Richmond was another army. In tattered trousers and ragged shirts, cheeks stubbled, eyes glittering with fires last stoked more than a century ago. Running, bounding over houses, rocketing through trees, the more disciplined ones lining up on the ridge line between us and the bottomland as officers waved swords and yelled.

"Hey, you! Where do you think you're going?"

"Calverton, I can see you behind that rock. Get over here."

"No, no, no, Simpson. Wait till he finishes puking. Then drag him along."

"Exactly what are you grinning at, soldier? You find something amusing here, Mr. Lechter?"

"If anyone sees any real soldiers, please tell them the war is waiting for them."

The valiant words, the rattle of musketry and the occasional *blat* of a bugle — it was humbling to know you once had a first-life filled with moments of such nobility. It made me thankful I now spent my time in a place where, if you say *recruiter*, ninety-seven spooks out of a hundred will think you're talking about an overly-zealous member of a 12-step program.

"What a sight," Shade said as he climbed back to the top of my pocket. "Makes you proud to be dead."

"If I hadn't had the breath taken out of me, it would be out of me now," I said.

Each puff of smoke spitting from an astral muzzle-loader was taking a pure, irreplaceable amount of ectoplasm from a rebel. But they fought on as though defending flag, honor and mom's key lime pie.

In the overcast moonless night, the rebel defenders of Richmond lined up in rows arcing around the southern flank of Libby Hill to the east. Discipline had somehow stumbled into the ranks, and, by and large, the troops held their fire until threatened by an officer brandishing a sword.

Volley after volley poured into the bottomland where Brother Randall's army was beginning to form into orderly ranks. I didn't see anyone from Randall's legions fall under the blistering fire, but they jerked back whenever the old Confederate firearms spoke up. Perhaps in reaction to the pinpricks of flame that bloomed from the muzzles of rifles, or the noise. Perhaps, because the ugly glances of the defenders were almost enough to persuade them to go away.

Eventually, weapons were lifted by the attackers: Randall's boys were cashing in their ectoplasm to show that they may not have proper backbones, but they still had guts.

Little puffs appeared on the hillside around me as spectral bullets raked the ground. Among Randall's people, someone had materialized an Uzi machine gun and tore the night with its buzzing fire. Even at a distance in the dark, I could see that stupid spook grow fainter and fainter as his ectoplasm spat furiously from the barrel of his weapon; within seconds, only the Uzi was visible; then it hung alone in the dark sputtering; then it fell, burping a round or two; then it was silent; then it was gone.

"Hey, guys," Gwendolyn yelled. "They're sneaking around the side. That away."

I ran with Hank to check out the exposed flank, my nostrils tricked into smelling the warm breath of gunpowder. A bullet hummed in front of me. Then a pain like an ice pick pierced my side. I staggered, slid down the hillside, clutching my chest. I stayed on my feet and by the time I realized that I'd been shot, the pain was gone.

No wounds, no blood, no ectoplasmic damage. And no great desire to repeat the experience anytime soon.

I ran past the cheering group surrounding Randall at the obelisk; it was clear a force of considerable size was working its way around our hill, out of sight of the defending rebels. If anyone heard Gwendolyn's warning, they hadn't bothered to heed it. Hundreds of glowing figures inched silently toward our position with the creepy stealth that made *ghostly* a bad word.

I looked at Hank and Gwendolyn. "Anyone interested in pooling together some ectoplasm?"

"Three guns won't stop that gang. It'll only annoy them," Hank said.

"How about three machine guns?" Gwendolyn's eyes were wide and glistening. "Or three tanks?"

I said, "You guys are thinking small."

Gwendolyn's cigar bobbed at me. "And the big thinker is thinking —?"

"Nukes."

I like it when a spook's jaw drops. If the light's right and the wind is from the north, you can see right down their gullets and get an inside look at the tops of their feet.

"I think I've got a better idea," Shade said.

"Out with it."

"I'm thinking of a bird. A very large bird. Okay, a colossal bird. Maybe even bigger than colossal."

Gwendolyn and Hank scoffed. Shade giggled. And I turned slowly to look over my shoulder at the city.

Slowly down the center of Main Street, stepping gingerly over the highway overpass, was a raven. A very big raven. A raven that was bigger than colossal. A raven that would have to stoop to become colossal.

CHAPTER Sixteen

andall's followers didn't need to see a Confederate uniform on the raven to know which side the bird was on. Have you ever wondered what the noise made by several thousand spooks going *poof* at the same second would sound like? Just imagine yourself standing in a railway station when four trains arrive at the same time on different tracks while a thunderstorm breaks loose during an earthquake.

Then imagine cranking up the volume.

The specters attacking from the eastern woods, the southern river and the southwestern edges of the city departed from Richmond with a boom that shook loose every dental filling in a four-county area. But a few of Randall's follow-ers — termed, in the technical lingo, *die-hard cases* — held their ground, and some even inched closer to the hill, while the faithful from the St. Sears meeting cheered like idiots for the raven and the boys in gray.

Around the base of the rebel monument, all of Randall's spooks must have remembered appointments they were late for, including Gilda and the other Cal. And the great Randall himself, floating nearly level with the statue on the obelisk, jabbed an accusing finger at the giant raven and said, "You'll be sorry," before *poofing* away.

If I could come up with snappy one-liners like that, I'd have my own mass movement, too.

Soon a blanket of darkness settled on the lowlands and spooks in tattered gray trudged to the top of Libby Hill. Slump-shouldered and heavy-lidded, they had something special that marked them as the winners of a great victory, a clearness in their eyes maybe, or perhaps the set of their chins.

In ragged columns they came, stacked their weapons and lay down on the grass to gaze into the starless sky. They'd had enough activity for one night. Somewhere in the distance, a harmonica took up a mournful melody, hushed conversations began, campfires broke out among the troops.

I can't explain the campfires. On the astral plane? Really! But there they were, flickering flames, glowing embers, potatoes cooking on the ashes, somebody's dog warming herself next to a fire.

Wait a minute. That's my dog.

"Petey," I called. "Petey, over here."

All wagging ears and flapping tongue, the beagle scampered over, then circled my ankles a few times to make sure I was all there. It's a good afterlife.

Hank and Gwendolyn approached the soldiers at the closest campfire.

"That's some weapon you got there," Gwendolyn said. "You ever think of cutting down the barrel? So's it'll fit in a trench coat without drawing a crowd?"

"Can't say I have." The Confederate soldier removed a hay stem from his mouth and eyed Gwendolyn coolly. Hay? What are these spooks doing with material gewgaws?

I haven't known Gwendolyn long, but this was the first time I saw him look awkward. Like a sixteen-year-old at a high school dance, he was all elbows and knees and glassy eyes and a hopeless stammer. And a cigar. He still had the stogie.

Hank pointed at the rifle that lay on the grass beside another soldier. "Can I... you know... if it's alright and all... can I hold it?"

This soldier didn't reply. Instead, he looked up with an expression that was halfway toward falling asleep and the other half about to slap Hank silly.

"Well," Hank said, "maybe later."

"You do that," the reb answered.

I steered Hank and Gwendolyn toward a less testy region of the hill where Darleen was waving at me.

"We won didn't we?" she called.

"With a little help from our friends." I nodded at the raven who was now directly in front of us.

"But they're not playing fair," Rosetta added, glancing down the ridge. "We won, but they aren't leaving."

I looked down the side of Libby Hill into the flood plains below and toward the wooded horizon in the south and east.

Sure enough, several hundred glowing figures were slowly floating up the hillside, their spectral hands clutching rifles, pistols and, for one Biblically inspired spook, a slingshot.

"May Day, May Day," I screamed and waved at the rebels lounging around the monument. "Bandits at twelve o'clock. May Day."

You'd think I was talking in a foreign language from the reaction I got from the exhausted troops.

"Let me try," Gwendolyn said, nudging me aside.

Before he could take the cigar from his mouth, a cataclysmic *caw, caw* shook the night, and the monster-raven, with surprising delicacy, probed the tree line with the tip of its beak. The ebony head lifted, the bird's eyes the red of fresh lava; something was clutched in its beak. Something glowing and writhing.

A spook. The bird had a spook.

The last of Randall's followers weren't frightened by a fusillade from a dead army or a ten-story reminder of Edgar A-'s greatest hit. But the sight of a giant monster having a midnight snack with one of their buddies, now that offended their sensibilities. They were gone faster than the twitch of a gnat's nose.

As the raven lumbered toward the hill, the poor soul clenched in its beak twisted in eerie silence. I don't suppose it would have been any consolation for that fellow to know that he was within hailing distance of a dozen members of Specters Anonymous. If he had to be lunch meat for a gigantic bird, he couldn't have planned things any better, for we'd make sure the story of his agony fueled 12-step meetings for decades.

The bird wobbled closer. I guess it was one of those creatures that didn't like to eat alone. Darleen and Rosetta squealed and zipped behind the obelisk. Which goes to show that you can take the spirit out of the girl, but you'll never get rid of the girl inside the spirit.

With a muted cough, the bird leaned over us and spat out the spook.

A few rebel soldiers watched the spook tumble from the raven's mouth, but the rest found nothing unusual in either a bird the size of Rhode Island or a fellow second-lifer who fell from the skies after being ejected from the animal's dinner menu.

The plunging spook landed with respectable agility on the grounds of Libby Hill. His hands flung upward in a dramatic fashion.

I heard him say, in a voice that was more familiar than I'd like it to be: "Quoth the raven."

The bird looked down, twisted its head to study the spook with one eye, then the other. It bent lower to wipe the sides of its beak on the grass.

"I said," said the new arrival, who was no less a local celebrity than Edgar Allan Poe, "Quoth the raven."

The bird flicked its beak through the feathers of its dark, dark breast, preening.

"Quoth the goddam raven!"

Edgar A- ascended to eye-level with the beast. "Look, my friend, I know you've had little opportunity to appreciate literature. I hope to remedy that deficiency later. For the moment, the task before us is to have you say, simply, *Nevermore*. Do you think you can handle it?"

The raven bobbed its head, and I'll give Poe credit for keeping his temper and trying to relate to the problem from the bird's perspective. If I could only persuade him to hold onto a sliver of that patience and tolerance around me.

"Quoth the raven," Poe thundered.

And the bird replied, "Whatever."

Poe tried for an hour to persuade the animal to take orders. I guess one of the perks of having a beak is that it's difficult for folks to lead you around by the nose. In fact, the longer Edgar A- worked on the raven, the less respect he got. Finally, the bird turned its back to the poet and shed a few house-sized servings of raven poop. Poe took it in stride; after all, he used to be a literary critic himself.

By then, the rebel army had decamped, and I'm sure most of the spooks in gray were cruising frat row on Hamilton Street. Cal — or more properly, the part of Cal that was left after some of him slipped away with Randall — sidled between two clumps of raven droppings and hovered next to me.

"I'm making a transcendence check," he said. "How's yours holding up?"

"Frankly, it's a bit shaky."

"You know what you should do when your recovery gets shaky?"

"Might it be," I hazarded, "the same thing I should do if I find myself surrounded by Galapagos turtles who are out of their minds on some wicked kelp and they're barreling down on me in a thundering herd?"

"The very same." Cal managed a smile, but it seemed to cost him something. "Find a spook who's struggling with recovery and help him."

"Or her."

"Him." Cal lost his battle to hold onto the smile.

Hank joined the discussion. "Got any ideas, boss, where we can find some fresh newbies at this time of night?"

Cal turned slightly and gazed at the distant highway overpasses. If I had been sitting in his eyeballs, I couldn't get a clearer picture of what he was looking at — the brick tower of the train station.

"Some of our spooks hitting the rails now, huh?" Gwendolyn asked.

Gwendolyn was more Cal's equal than anyone else at St. Sears, with the possible exception of Rosetta, even though Gwendolyn was a newbie and Cal had so many years in recovery I doubt he remembered what the heat of the sun felt like. But Cal couldn't even muster the energy to look Gwendolyn in the eye when he shook his head.

Cal wasn't going to be able to take many more nights of Randall. That slick-talking specter had managed to wedge a kernel of doubt into Cal's indomitable soul. Maybe Specters Anonymous wasn't the best way to put together time in the afterlife. Maybe everything Cal had learned — and taught others — about transcendence was wrong. For every spook that Cal had helped in recovery, perhaps a dozen more had been driven into the sunshine by useless advice.

I felt a dull, frightening, lumpish kind of grief. Not pain that can sink its teeth into my ectoplasm, but loss that will drain the color from the night. Grief that announced its arrival long before it dusted off its hat and waited patiently for someone to answer its knock at the front door.

Petey had joined us. Although she hadn't met Cal before, she watched my sponsor with an intensity that I'd only seen in those warm, chocolate eyes when they were staring at me. Petey lifted her paw, and for a moment I thought the dog was going to pet the spook. But the beagle rocked back on her haunches, uncertain whether to sit or stand or scamper away, sensing that something about Cal was unlike any other specter she'd met.

I sensed it, too. It was the aura of a spook who would be soon, as we say, *riding the wind*, as everything that made him unique and vital blended into the oceans and the desert sands and the voids between stars.

Seventeen
CHAPTER

s we were leaving Libby Hill, Shade allowed as how his nook in the drainage pipe wasn't far, and he'd appreciate it if someone could take him back to there before it got too late and, since he had at least three hundred and eighty-seven questions to ask about the Specters Anonymous program, he was wondering if Cal wouldn't mind giving him a lift.

For a specter who could fit on a three-by-five index card with space left for a casserole recipe, Shade was pretty sharp.

"Anything to help a fellow spook," Cal replied. A glimmer of the old Cal returned when Shade hopped from my shirt pocket and crawled underneath Cal's collar.

Cal took a last glance at the distant railway station, looked at me, then sauntered off with Shade.

"The boss don't look too good," Hank said as the pair drifted away.

"Maybe Cal can bunk with Shade tonight," Gwendolyn added. "I'd hate to think of him being... you know."

"Yeah, I know," I said. "*Alone* or *by himself*. Maybe even, *in a place where he might stumble across a grow-light*."

Gwendolyn lifted his well-chewed stogie and spat. "Nah, I was thinking about him not having anyone around for a card game. When I get to looking like that, I need a couple hours of poker to put the color back in my cheeks."

I tried to picture Gwendolyn with rosy cheeks and failed. Not even as a toddler could I imagine Gwendolyn with rosy cheeks. For that matter, the only mental pictures of him as a child that I could summon all included the cigar stub.

Hank leaned across me to ask Gwendolyn, "What kind of color of cheeks are we talking about here?"

"Ash."

"Oh, that's alright then."

The railroad station that Cal wanted us to check for newbies was a sturdy brick building that had seen better centuries. By the standards of a major city, it was small, with a single ticket counter now able to handle the trade.

"What are we looking for?" Gwendolyn asked.

"Anyone who looks as confused as you felt when you first showed up here."

"I'm on it."

The three of us split up, zipped through every room, hallway, storage closet, garbage can, cabinet, closet, fuse box, tool chest, water pipe, heating duct and sewage drain, and eventually met on the sloping roof of the building's clock tower.

"Zero," Gwendolyn said.

"Nada," Hank added.

"Nothing," I elaborated.

"Maybe Cal was wrong about newbies being here?" Hank said.

"If Cal were cooked on a beach until he looked like the ghost of a lobster, he still wouldn't be wrong about something like that," I said.

I scanned the cityscape, then brought my search closer. Directly below us, a dozen spooks — a few couples, but mostly loners — loitered on benches beside the tracks. An advantage of post-mortality is that you don't have to use public transportation any more. But many newbies don't have confidence in their ability to employ the *Beam-Me-up-Scotty* method of getting around, so you'll always find a few on most trains, planes and cross-country buses.

Behind the station was an area covering most of a city block where the business of keeping a railroad running used to be done. Now it was home to a field of concrete.

And something else. A low, narrow building of weather-beaten wood and sun-dried tarpaper. Drifting along the front of the building were a couple spooks who, if this weren't the afterlife where the residents were coming to grips with their first lives and preparing for whatever came after this one, I'd describe as guards.

"Is it me or is the smell of hair grease coming from that place?" Gwendolyn asked.

"I don't remember Cal saying we can't get newbies who've been gotten by someone else," Hank said. "What do you think?"

"I've seen the dark, brothers," I answered. "The sunshine has lifted, the twilight has fallen, and I have seen the dark."

We transformed ourselves into three dispirited spirits who slunk out of the train station moments later and ambled across the concrete courtyard. From time to time, I'd look squarely into one of the street lamps that illuminated the area and flap my hands in front of my face. Urging the feeble light not to waste time before it reached me.

Gwendolyn limped and moaned. Hank hummed the *Battle Hymn of the Republic*.

"Halt." A spook by the outbuilding held his hands in front of his chest as though gripping a rifle, although, since he wasn't gripping a rifle, any authority the specter had came from our fear of being around a nut. "Who goes there?"

"Three recruits for Brother Randall's army."

From the side of his mouth, Hank whispered, "This ought to double their fighting power."

"What's the password?"

I traded a look with Gwendolyn, he passed it along to Hank who, seeing as how it was my look in the first place, returned it to me.

I said the first thing that wanted to get out of my mouth: "Lonesome no more."

"Close enough." Grandly, the guard gestured us through the door. "Welcome to the only path to righteousness, brothers."

As we passed inside, Hank whispered, "How'd you know the password?"

"I didn't" was my whispered reply. "That was just the first thing that popped into my head."

Gwendolyn turned to the guard. "Brother, I may have to leave in a few minutes on important transcendental business involving slot machines for the new Happily-Ever-After Resort, could you tell me the exact password?"

"The password is *fried water chestnuts*."

Hank rolled his eyes. Gwendolyn almost threw down his cigar. But one doesn't bring a stogie into the afterlife if one is inclined to throw it away at every little act of insanity.

"How is *fried water chestnuts* close enough to *lonesome no more?*" Gwendolyn asked.

"It's not." The guard was baffled by the question. "It's just that your friend seemed so sincere about *lonesome no more.*"

"I knew there was a good reason," Gwendolyn said.

The inside of the building was a region of fog and shadows. Drifting from the door, I expected to reach the rear wall immediately, but I turned back after a minute of coasting through a thin gray gruel of air.

Hank and Gwendolyn hovered by the door, each wearing an expression of confusion with a heavy layer of fear. Which suited my own reaction to a shiver. Randall's place was like nothing else I'd seen on this side of the Great Divide. Like nothing should be on this side.

In an alcove near the entrance, grow-lights hung from the ceiling near a metal fence. At least, it would be a metal fence if it were made of metal instead of this freaky fog. The grow-lights flashed on, several dozen spooks on the other side of the fence rushed toward the light, but the fence kept them from touching it.

"What the hey?" Gwendolyn said.

"This is a repo," I answered confidently. "A repossessed structure. A paranormal manifestation in a paranormal world. After you've sorted out all the *para's*, it means this place acts like a house in the physical world. Unfortunately, it also means we act as if we're in the physical world when we're here."

"Does that mean I gotta look out for skulls dropping from the ceiling?" Hank hitched up his spectral belt.

"Be afraid," I answered. "Be very afraid."

One snarky remark deserves another, but before Hank could get his out, a female voice cut through the gloom.

"Ralph, party of three. Mr. Ralph, party of three."

Time spent on two planes of existence didn't prepare me for the owner of that voice. I've known people who had *efficiency* written all over them. This creature could have had *struggling to be competent* emblazoned in neon above her eyes.

She introduced herself as Mrs. Pellywanger. She was clad in a smock that resembled a medieval monk's tunic. Her face was an amalgam of fleshy rolls that threatened to unite into a single ball of flab with eyes, ears and a diminishing nose.

She had a clipboard in her hands that showered pages when she moved, a pencil and a pen behind her left ear, a wedge of chalk and the nub of a crayon pressed into her hair on the right side, and paperclips clinging to whatever was available. She was, like Margie, a *two-fer*, a resident of the material world who had a visitor's pass for the afterlife.

From beneath her smock poked two feet with sandals, both generally nondescript, if it hadn't been for the large yellow ribbon tied around a big toe.

Mrs. Pelly noticed my interest in her toe.

"It's supposed to help me remember," she said.

"Does it work?"

"It's wonderful, just amazing," Mrs. Pelly said, staring at her own beribboned toe. "Everyone says so."

In the alcove on the other side of the hall, the grow-lights switched off amid a chorus of moans and whines, even the occasional catcall.

"What's that about?" I asked.

Mrs. Pelly looked up from her feet. "That's the *A* version of some risky therapy."

Time spent with Gilda and Margie enabled me to sense the tidal sweep of Mrs. Pelly's thoughts. "Would that be *risk aversion therapy?*"

"That's what I said." Her smile was hopeful. "But I think it confuses spooks to talk about the *A-version* in one fast clip. Especially when nobody's heard of the *B-version*. You gotta put a little space between some words where the mind has the room to wrap itself around some ideas, I always say."

"I was about to say the very same thing," I offered, "if I'd thought of it."

Hank straightened his shoulders. Gwendolyn considered the dark point of his stogie. If this were a place where brute force counted for anything, I'd feel safer.

"Do you know," I asked Mrs. Pelly, "the difference between aversion therapy and torture?"

"Nah," Mrs. Pelly said, all aglow. "I haven't heard that one yet."

"The difference is the amount of blood on the lab coats of the people in charge."

"Ha, ha." Mrs. Pelly was polite but puzzled. She looked at me. "I don't get it."

"It's a translation from the Chinese. Only funny if you're from Singapore."

"That explains it then. Lab coat, ha." She ran her finger down rows of scrib-blings in pen, pencil, crayon and chalk on her clipboard. "Ralph, party of three."

I raised a finger. "Here."

"Follow me, please."

Shedding scraps of paper and paperclips, Mrs. Pelly led us further into the miasma of fog and shadows. Like a true repo, the place had a mind of its own: sometimes we filed through tunnels in the fog, sometimes through tunnels chipped from gray rock, and sometimes through tunnels flickering between the material and the nonmaterial worlds. Always out of sight were indistinct, mur-muring voices and the rustling of smocks dragged on the ground.

Mrs. Pelly kept up a stream of conversation with figures who materialized on the edges of our procession:

"Toodle-oo, there Mildred. You sleeping any better in that new bucket?... My best to the missus, Samuel.... Oh, Billy, that was some charge you led at the raven tonight. You almost had him.... Don't worry, dearie, next time we'll all know to look out for the droppings."

The further we advanced into the repo, the more I realized how large and empty it was. This was a place that Randall had sought to house an army. Specifically, the army of spooks who had tried to storm the city, wipe out all traces of Specters Anonymous and impose their own version of transcendence.

A memory wriggled in a dark, distant reach of my mind. "I'm trying to remember an old story. Something about houses found empty, dinner plates on the table, the family car in the garage. And the family is never seen again."

Gwendolyn actually removed the cigar from his mouth in a rare moment of excitement. "Yeah, I heard there were plane crashes, especially in the olden days when regular folks were just starting to fly. Crashes where nobody ever found no bodies."

"Ask them about Marie Celeste." Without warning, Gilda was at my side. "The food was warm in the kitchen."

"Gilda, wait a minute. What are you talking about?"

"You don't want to know what they think about blueberries and chocolate here."

"Blueberries?"

"And Culchu," she added, as her features dissolved into a wisp of fog. "Pin them down about Culchu."

In the next instant, she was gone.

$\mathscr{Eighteen}$
CHAPTER

"Ahem," I asserted to Mrs. Pellywanger. She was leading Hank, Gwendolyn and me through another interminable tunnel of fog and gray rock. "Would you happen to have a Mary Celeste here?"

"That one does have a certain familiarity. Unfortunately—" here she waved the clipboard and created a blizzard of twirling papers "—our records system is being updated as we speak."

"How about Culchu," Hank offered. "Not sure if that's a first name or a last name."

"Why, that's neither." Mrs. Pelly was as bright as a spring morning. "That was an ancient Indian city, somewhere around St. Louis. Wonderful work with blankets and ceramics."

Ceramics. That rang a chime.

"What happened to it?" I asked.

"Oh, they're here," our guide said brightly. "Least ways, they will be soon. Brother Randall is working on a way around that dreadful raven. Wasn't it dreadful?"

"Dreadful," Hank echoed.

"Could Mary Celeste be a city like Culchu?" I shot into the dark.

Mrs. Pelly stopped and grinned at me. Her many-chinned face was on the verge of ripping in two. "Ah, now I remember. Not a city nor a person, gracious no. *Mary Celeste* was a boat. One of those nasty things with sails and rats. They're with us, too."

"When you say *with us*, you mean——"

She jabbed the foggy air with her clipboard. "Third tunnel to the left. Take the first right, then the second left, then introduce yourself."

"And who would I be introducing myself to?"

"The passengers and crew of the *Mary Celeste*."

We followed Mrs. Pelly for another five minutes before she said, "Wait here," and stepped off into the foggy shadows.

I fought the urge to flit from one side of the corridor to the other, owing to this feeling that I was inside a dust-bag that was attached to a cosmic vacuum cleaner. No one ever goes missing in the afterlife, it seems. They just show up at Brother Randall's.

"Good thing Gilda tipped us off about the *Mary Celeste* and that Indian village," Gwendolyn said. "Saved me a couple nights of intensive investigation to figure out where Brother Randall thought he'd get enough spooks to fill this funhouse."

"Yeah," I said. "Real nice of her." I paused. "Why should she want to do us any favors?"

Hank's eyes darted from side to side. "Maybe things will look clearer from someplace with trees and grass. Beam me up, Scotty."

Poof. He was gone. *Poof.* He was back, floating near the ground, rubbing his head.

"Like I said earlier," I pointed out, "a repossessed house makes us —— and everything around us —— behave like we're still breathers."

"Everything?" Hank asked.

My last encounter with a repo included water pipes that tried to strangle me, electrical wires that wanted to hang me, walls that did their darndest to crush me, and the airborne contents of several kitchen drawers that tried to slice and dice me.

"Well, it's just like a real house, except for the bits that aren't," I retorted.

"Clear enough for me," said Gwendolyn.

And that's another thing. Why am I looking for protection and advice from a cigar-chewing spook with the physique of a truck tire who goes by the name of Gwendolyn? Or a lady-killer who hangs around with ladies who've already been killed or otherwise shown to their own caskets?

I felt a long-delayed rant coming on. A lie-down-on-your-tummy-and-kick-your-feet tantrum.

Before I could unloosen my inner toddler, the darkness and the fog started talking to us. Perhaps *talking* isn't the best description. More like a bad marriage between a hiss and a growl.

Hank and Gwendolyn turned slowly, their fists clenched, their eyes tore through the gloom. We met in the middle of the hall with our backs pressed into a three-way knot.

"You're going to be sorry if you start anything," I said to the mysterious noise.

"I already am," Hank replied.

The shadows wavered, the fog rippled, then shadow and fog merged into a single form that glided toward me with mumbled murmurs that sounded almost thoughtful. Behind it came another creature with the same featureless concoction of gray darkness, then another, then a fourth.

The first one was close enough for me to make out the folds and cowl of a monk's robe. I grabbed the hood and threw it aside. And found myself staring into a distillation of the sky. Blue and warm, distant yet gracious and benevolent.

"Nevermore," said Miss Blue Eyes, guide for the intrepid tour group from Cincinnati. She giggled. And all the other figures lined up in the dark behind her giggled.

"Good evening, Mr. Poe," she said.

An apology was in order. Perhaps an explanation. Maybe even a convincing lie. But by now several dozen spooks in the robes and hoods of monks were crowded around us in Mrs. Pelly's hall.

"What are you doing here?" I asked.

Miss Blue Eyes pursed her rosy lips in a painfully cute way and said, "We heard the ruckus on the hill earlier this evening. So we went to see what was going on."

"I got to be Johnny Reb," one of her companions said.

"I got to be a Yank," a second replied.

"I got to be a Crusader," a third said.

This last revelation was greeted with hoots and hisses and calls of, "You missed the point, Garrison."

"No, *you* missed the point," Garrison shot back.

Miss Blue Eyes smiled benignly, and I struggled to remember how my voicebox worked. "And you're with Brother Randall now?" I stammered.

"I wouldn't say that," she said. "But he had some really interesting ideas. We thought that if we can't be back in Cincinnati"— The foggy chamber rocked with a three-second burst of cheers —"then we should learn what we can while we're here."

Her cheery openness made me feel like specterdom's number one heel for creeping into Brother Randall's domain like a spy. As though he weren't just another spook who's trying to figure out why he's here and where he should be heading.

"Ralph, party of three. Mr. Ralph, party of three."

Mrs. Pelly was back, and Miss Blue Eyes favored me with a smile that ought to count as a stumblie under Specters Anonymous's no-sunshine rule. With a wave of her hand, she led her Ohioans further into Randall's lair. Someone — Garrison, I'll bet — was humming a Gregorian chant.

"You're in luck," said Mrs. Pelly. She had found more pieces of paper for her clipboard during her absence, which she now liberally sprayed throughout the cavern. "Brother Randall has an opening between a private meeting with the Most Grand Specter of Bangor and an audience with delegations visiting from the West Coast."

"Your Brother Randall sounds like he's been around the park," Hank said as we followed Mrs. Pelly.

"He does enjoy his moments outside, when his schedule allows," she answered brightly.

"And how long has he been dead?" I asked.

"Dead? How can you say such a thing? Especially about an entity who's doing so much for others?"

"How about yourself, Chickadee?" Gwendolyn must have thought things were going too smoothly. "When did you hit your expiration date?"

"I don't know what you mean?" Mrs. Pelly's round face quivered on the verge of collapse.

"When did they plant you?" Hank jumped in. "When'd you join the choir eternal? What's the date on your membership card for Specters Anonymous?"

"Ooooooh!" She threw her clipboard into the air and scurried away.

"How do we find Brother Randall?" I shouted.

"Straight ahead. Don't you people know how to read signs?"

As it turned out, I didn't need a sign to know when we reached Brother Randall's hangout. For most of his lair, fog and gray rock were transmuted into each other, then back again, without warning or pattern. Spooks flitted away at our approach, and I shuddered to imagine them slipping into the cold embrace of a stone wall that might never release them.

Brother Randall's place was distinctive. I guess it was the automatically opening glass doors that gave it away, although the plush orange carpets and subdued lighting helped.

The spook behind the receptionist's desk was outfitted in a no-nonsense business suit with a high collar that didn't quite obscure the fact that her neck was three or four times normal length.

Gwendolyn whistled. "And I thought I've seen bad face-lifts."

The receptionist shot Gwendolyn a look that should have knocked the old spook out of the afterlife, through his third and fourth lives, and right to the head of the line for those leaving their fifth lives.

"Ralph?" the receptionist asked.

"That's me."

"Go in." She jabbed a thumb over her shoulder at the rock wall and, head swaying on her gangly neck, dared Gwendolyn with her eyes to open his mouth. A lethal head butt was a twitch away.

With a cheery smile, I headed toward the wall, more willing to break my astral nose than to give her the satisfaction of showing fear. I mean, what's the worst that could happen? Other than being entombed for a couple millennia in a rock that was tired of pretending it was a fog bank.

But the wall was a patch of gray air when I reached it, and, accompanied by my two companions in recovery, I stepped without incident into a room where hundreds of spooks drifted slowly in two neat lines around the walls and out a door in back. Think of a viewing line at a funeral home threading its way past a casket. Then make the body vertical, long-winded, decked out in a hairdo the texture of Kevlar, and absorbed in a private conversation. That'll give you a picture of Brother Randall greeting the faithful.

A spook leaned over from his place in line and stuck out his hand. "Isn't this fabulous? I used to think *died and gone to heaven* was the most. But this is the absolute mostest."

I took the spook's hand. What else could I do?

"Yeah, the mostest," I said. "I'm embarrassed to admit this, but I don't know why I'm here. I mean, in this room."

"Don't worry about it, kid." He nudged me with an elbow. "Leaving the glow-bug life scrambles the best of us. Why, I have a buddy back home — it took us a decade to get him to stop jumping into every car he saw with keys in the ignition and trying to drive away."

He checked the line ahead, drifted forward a couple of inches, and continued brightly:

"Why are we here? Some of us — I mean, if we've very careful with our recoveries and avoid anything that smacks of the material world — are allowed to spend a few minutes in the presence of our great brother." Were those tears gathering in the spook's eyes? "I never thought I'd make it this far."

"Yeah, recovery's not for sissies."

"To be this close to Brother Randall. In the same room." Tears were now pouring down the old fellow's cheeks. "I am blessed."

"Look, why don't you sit down someplace and relax? You don't want to go spilling ectoplasm. There's no more of that where you've come from."

"I don't care. I'm in the presence of greatness."

Then his Greatness noticed me and my friends. "Come," he said. His voice was as chilly as a new iceberg. For he spoke without moving his lips. Like a ventriloquist, projecting his words at a dummy.

That would be me.

CHAPTER

wendolyn chewed his cigar like a ruminating bull, Hank rolled the sleeves of his black t-shirt to expose more of his spectral muscles, and I decided that I didn't have anything to prove here.

A real spook doesn't need to be right all the time. There's no shame in telling my friends I was having some sort of breakdown when they thought they heard me talk about sneaking into Brother Randall's place and poking around.

In fact, the literature of Specters Anonymous tells us to avoid *the people, places and things that lead to whacked-out notions of entertainment.*

I would have slunk away if one of the spooks talking to Randall hadn't shifted aside to let me see two glum faces in the background. Gilda and Cal, looking like a mismatched set of whipped puppies.

Instead, I drifted to the great leader and let myself do what came naturally under the circumstances. I prostrated myself at his feet and said, "I have come to learn the mysteries of the universe."

"You must prove you are worthy." Randall looked at me as though this sort of thing didn't happen every day. It happened several times an hour.

"Test me. Give me a quest."

"How about a pop quiz?"

I looked up. "Written or oral?"

"Short," the master replied. He reached down and pulled me upright. The power in his hands was astonishing. Each finger felt made of steel: even his knuckles had biceps.

"We must eradicate the errors of Specters Anonymous and their deluded followers," he said. "We must show them the only correct path to transcendence."

"*Deluded* is my middle name. What would you have me do, Most Lofty One?"

"I must know about the forces who opposed us this evening. How many of them are there? Where are they now? Are they spread across the city, or are they concentrated at certain spots."

Here I'd come to spy on him, and he wants me to spy on my friends. I didn't think I was in transcendence-land anymore.

"*Forces opposing us?*" I scoffed. "There are no forces, Your Uberness. Just gangs of spooks who've been drifting around the last one hundred and fifty years, hoping that something like this would happen."

"But they know about my followers. We have lost the advantage of surprise."

Gilda fixed her eyes on me. Slowly, beyond Randall's vision, she shook her head.

"Not true, your magnitude." Having put my foot in my mouth, I knew I couldn't rest until I had jammed it down into my stomach. "Like I said, they've been sitting around for decades. Sitting around is what they do best. What do you think they're expecting from you now?"

Randall arched his eyebrows. Gilda looked nervous, in a sluggish, zombie-like way. Cal studied the rock flecks on the floor.

I gulped and pushed ahead into the unknown: "What they're expecting from you... is... absolutely... without question... and in bright neon lights—" Sometimes inspiration falls from the heavens like rain, other times it's a clogged toilet, backing up into my brain. I studied the hopelessness, the lethargy, the lack of gristle in Cal's face and concluded: "NOTHING! And you should give them exactly that."

"What?" I swear little bolts of lightning caromed around the room when Randall raised his head. "What sort of advice is that?"

"The best advice," I stammered. Men with no necks were beginning to converge on their leader and the idiot who was upsetting him. "Your enemies have felt the might of your hand and have seen the darkness of your face. Yet they foolishly believe that you are crushed and defeated."

"It was the bird that did it," Randall said. All around him, heads began bobbing furiously, and I thought a bad face-lift might not be the only explanation for the receptionist's neck.

"When I was a kiddie, listening to that silly poem on my mother's knee, I knew I'd rather be on the Bataan Death March than hear one more *Nevermore*," Randall continued. "Even then I knew that devil bird had it in for me."

I found it easier to imagine Randall dancing with a purple lamp shade over his head than being a *kiddie*.

"In two days, maybe three, they will convince themselves that you are truly vanquished," I said.

Gwendolyn winced, Hank cringed, and I knew I was racing right into the astral quicksand. Both of those spooks knew more thugs than I did. I was afraid to look at Randall to see how badly I'd overstepped common sense.

"One day," I amended. "In one day, they will boast and bang their drums. They will let down their guard. They will celebrate. And in that moment, when they are convinced that you have left the field in defeat, they will be yours."

"And the bird?"

"I hear it tastes like chicken."

I leaned closer to Randall than prudence or good hygiene should allow and picked up the strangest scent. From my experience, among the advantages of dying is that you don't have to bathe, brush your teeth or gargle. After all, if you're immaterial, what's to pick up an odor that offends?

But Randall had a definite scent about him. Something earthy, like baked bread or mud drying in the sun.

He looked at me with eyes that were the smoldering red of the raven's and said, "We will talk more about this when you give me what I seek."

"Absolutely, Your Worshipfulness. If you want to smite the enemies of enlightenment, I'm your tool."

I followed Gilda out of the audience chamber and into another interminable length of fog and tunnels chiseled from gray stone. Gwendolyn and Hank were behind us, pumping Cal for suggestions about having a good time in this joint.

Gilda stopped me with an upraised hand, slowly checked the area, and let me have it. "It passes all understanding that you could have been dead this long. You think you can toy with Randall? That spook knows more dirty tricks than anyone else has thought about. *It tastes like chicken, Your Worshipfulness.* Give me a break."

"This from Miss Holy-and-Sunshine-Free. Who never dreamed of tasting blueberries soaked in caramel."

"I would die again for caramel."

Lesson one for dealing with dead Goths: Admissions of weakness and moments of indecision are rare, so if one ever comes along, drive a sixteen-wheeler into that breach as soon as possible.

"Is the most self-confident spirit in two planes of existence saying that she made a mistake?" I asked. "Had a change of heart?"

"Not on your death." Gilda went quickly from serious to all business. I know that doesn't sound like much of a change, but with Gilda I've learned to savor every hint of an emotion.

"The first time I heard Brother Randall's brand of hooey, I knew the spook was dangerous," she said. Even without a quarter-pound of eyeliner and makeup, Gilda was all Goth. "I've been playing along with him. Seeing what he's up to, so that we can stop him."

"Well, what do you think I'm doing?" I growled.

One of the nicest things Gilda ever did to me was keep her mouth shut for the next five seconds. One of the nastiest things involved the look on her face during that period.

"Stopping Randall — Is that the only reason you had?" she finally asked.

"Well, I had this stupid idea about impressing someone."

It would be difficult to say whether Gilda or I was more surprised by the words that meandered out of my mouth.

She dealt with the revelation in classic Goth fashion. She refused to acknowledge that anything said within the last thirty seconds could have the remotest interest to her.

"We've got to know more about Brother Randall," she finally said. "Who he really is, where he came from, how he managed to put together an army. Absolutely everything."

I tried my best Sam Spade imitation. "Listen here, sister. You just turned up aces. With you and me on the case —"

"No." Gilda paused. She gave the rock wall a look that should have reduced it to lava before continuing: "I'll stay close to Brother Randall. You need to find out what you can. And quickly."

I was about to ask if that would impress her, and I might have, if the glance she flicked my way hadn't had a trace of pleading in it.

Gilda left to take her attitude for a walk. Cal drifted up the hall with Hank and Gwendolyn.

"Guys, you'll never guess what I learned about Gilda," I told them.

Gwendolyn's cigar stood at full attention. The corners of Hank's eyes crinkled with amusement: he'd thought for some time that Gilda's Goth lifestyle was on the verge of collapse and was looking forward to the grand implosion.

Cal studied me with the hollow eyes of a stranger.

"What gives, great spook," Hank said.

I looked at my three friends. I would trust Hank and Gwendolyn with my transcendence. But Cal? I didn't know about Cal anymore.

"Gilda said that, er, she thinks she's allergic to black leather," I stammered.

"I think she's allergic to her own shadow," Hank said.

"We don't have shadows, old hoss," Gwendolyn offered.

Enough of Cal — the old Cal, the original, undivided Cal — remained to put a stop to gossip between the members of the St. Sears group.

"Why don't I show you the buckets you can have tonight?" Cal asked. "If they're not to your liking, we can always look for something else."

"Give me a rain check on that," Gwendolyn said. "I think I want to poke around."

"Me, too," Hank said.

Cal didn't say anything as he led me through a corridor of maybe-fog-maybe-rock, then another, and yet more ahead. Even in the gloomy half-light, I could tell the pull that Randall exerted on Cal's loyalty to Specters Anonymous was strong.

It all came down to one question.

"Are you happy?" I asked him.

"Yes." Cal paused. "No." Another pause. "Dunno. What do you think?"

"About me being happy?'

"No," Cal said. "Me."

We didn't share another word as we wound through the darkness and the muffled glow that was more a rumor of light than light itself. When Cal stopped, I needed a moment or two to get my bearings.

We were in a cavern or a hallway, narrow, with a low ceiling and lined with squat earthen pitchers that reminded me of the demented work of Letitia Sanderling in the brownstone that Margie's Psychic Advisory Service shared with storage rooms for legal files, a tanning salon and the ugliest ashtray in this (or any other) universe, populated by two of the afterlife's least pleasant personalities.

Well, any empty bucket before sunup was a good bucket.

I was heading toward the ceramic containers in an alcove, when Cal touched my arm. Cal's ectoplasm was decomposing: he felt like a tree limb that had been sitting so long under water that the pulp was squishy.

"You know," I said, "maybe Brother Randall is right. There's nothing wrong with following your best judgment. You won't even lose any friends at the St. Sears group."

Cal's smile was wan.

"You don't know what you want to believe in, do you?" I asked. "Specters Anonymous or Brother Randall?"

"No." An ashen light flickered on Cal's face. "But I'm sure of one thing."

"What's that?"

"That I want to be sure of one thing."

What do you do when the wisest spook on this side of the Great Divide reveals that he has feet of ectoplasm? Cal was as vulnerable as anyone else drifting through happily-ever-after, wondering when he'd learn to play the harp. A true friend would nudge him back to the wisdom of the *Teeny Book* and the magic that comes to bare basement rooms when a few scared, puzzled, clueless specters decide they'd rather show their weaknesses than face the sunshine alone.

But what if Specters Anonymous is wrong? Or if it's generally right, but wrong for the likes of Cal? What the Roth! What if Brother Randall is full of lies, danger and self-deception, but he makes Cal happy?

"Maybe things will look different in the twilight." I poked a leg into one of the big ceramic pots.

"No!" Cal stared at the pot, daring it to move.

I may spend my spare time with corpses, but this situation was getting too freaky for me. I eased away from the pot.

"Look, if it's your bucket —"

Cal was frightened.

"Or Mr. Big's —" I added.

Now Cal's face was stony.

It was my turn to stare at that pot as Cal led me further down the hallway. Of the hundreds of containers I'd seen in this place, it was by far the ugliest. Asymmetrical, with a surface that looked like a bad case of eczema, and dyed a color that reminded me of a drunkard's nose — it was bad enough to fit into the collection of Letitia Sanderling.

And that's the one Brother Randall wanted for himself.

As I said to myself the night I rematerialized in an industrial-sized vat of soiled baby diapers: *Something here smells funny.*

CHAPTER Twenty

hat are the odds that pieces of cooked clay would become important in several different contexts within a few nights? I can't recall ever thinking much about tinfoil. Or a wooden baseboard or a plastic pipe. Okay, maybe the pipe isn't a good example: I've had issues with the plumbing in a couple of repossessed buildings lately.

But ceramics were involved in Randall's bizarre sleeping-pot and the ashtray that had somehow imprisoned Margie's reluctant (and noisy) guests.

Before I could check out that angle, however, a more immediate concern that sprang from something Randall said during his worship session needed my attention.

With no more effort than a wispy spore launching into the wind from a dandelion, I sent myself cruising through the hallways of Randall's Spirit Emporium and Hokum Warehouse, out the door and back to Libby Hill and the obelisk for the city's Confederate defenders.

The monument was deserted and the only light came from an arc of houses along its northern side and parts of the eastern and western. Barely a block away was Petey's home. The strong coffee aroma of the old hobo's pot where I'd bunked for several weeks called to me, and for a moment I was tempted to spend the day there. My investigation of ceramics could wait until tomorrow night.

Before I could head down the familiar, tree-lined street to the house over-looking the flood plain, I saw a solitary figure in gray near the obelisk.

"Halt. Who goes there?" he asked.

"Nobody special," I answered.

"Well, then, you ought to be alright."

His gray uniform had a rigid, high collar, bulging side pockets and sleeves with soiled embroidery. His hair was thin and gray, his face lined from a first life spent outdoors, and his eyes sparkled with a keenness that subtracted fifteen years from his age.

"Has it been quiet here?" I asked. "I mean since the battle?"

"It's never quiet after a battle, son." His accent was refined. This was a spook who, as a man, probably never put on a pair of shoes that didn't have a fresh shine, and I could see a trace of sadness for the lowered standards he'd had to accept in his second life.

"A few enemy patrols had the notion of probing our perimeter," he added, "but I chased them off. Even troops whose ears are still ringing from musket and cannon fire can be scared off by a madman. Trick is to come at them hollering and whooping and jumping up and down."

"I'll bet you jump well," I said.

"In my younger days, I was quite the terror around children and small dogs."

That broke the ice. We stood on the ridge line and, to the west, saw the city glow with street lamps, buildings, even the occasional car or truck trundling down the streets. To the east, where woodlands prevail and the James River curved abruptly to follow the falling terrain to the ocean, the darkness held a tight grip on the land.

For most of the details of my first life — like my occupation, home, family, name — my astral hard drive has been wiped clean and re-formatted, but I'm pretty sure I haven't spent any time in uniform. Despite that, something about the situation that night on Libby Hill seemed obvious. (*Note on cultural sensitivity: Avoid the phrase no brainer around any specter unless you're absolutely sure his first life wasn't spent in ancient Egypt.*)

"Aren't we a little thin, defense-wise?" I asked.

"We'll be fine for the rest of the night."

"You're a futurarian?" I said, and to a puzzled look expanded: "Someone who knows what's going to happen?"

"Ain't no kind of *'arian* unless you count *pragmatarian*," was the calm answer. "They won't be coming with only a few hours of darkness left. No time to consolidate their position if they manage to take the hill, no time to readjust if they don't. So, we're fine — for now. Come the twilight, though, I suspect we'll be up to our ears with new arrivals. And I'm not talking about tourists."

"I'll sleep better this morning knowing that," I said.

The colonel — for I couldn't imagine a lesser rank on one who took so matter-of-factly the rattle of musketry in this second life — started drifting away, his eyes studying the lowland approaches. If I was going to learn what I came here for, I had to act now.

What was Randall's exact phrase? That he'd been a child *sitting on his mother's knee* who'd rather be on the Bataan Death March than listen to her read Poe's *The Raven*. Since the infamous death march was in the early 1940s and spooks rarely assumed the form of someone older than they were at death, that would place Randall's earliest expiration date around the turn of the last century.

"What would you say," I asked the colonel, "if I told you the enemy commander has been gathering his army for a few decades?"

"I'd say you must have swallowed some of that bird pie that fell from the clouds this evening. No way a soul can touch that many spooks — get them fired up and moving in the same direction — in so little time."

The colonel gazed into the darkness, and I was sure he saw things I could never imagine. He added: "Then again, how does any of us know what's normal here? Our kind don't have a nodding acquaintance with *normal*."

My next stop was the Richmond Fine Arts Center, a brick structure planted — appropriately enough — between downtown and Carytown. Between money and funk.

Low fog had rolled in from the river, and some of the local artists were busy at work on the grounds. By the front door I saw a replica of Mona Lisa emerge from the mists, her cryptic smile now reworked into a full-toothed, beauty contestant's grin, although the details about her dress, hair and the mysterious figures in the background were faithfully rendered.

Those background figures, by the way, according to a spook I ran into who hung out with Leonardo when they both enjoyed a good sun tan, were in fact a cleverly designed code. Unfortunately, if you had the key, you'd realize the code was about Leonardo's wife's birthday. Great painter? — absolutely. Good memory for birthdays and anniversaries? — not on your afterlife.

Mona's smile widened when she saw me. I've always had this effect upon anyone sprinkled with estrogen.

The other works in progress included a couple Jackson Pollock smorgasbords, a few landscapes of the view from the lawn, some nifty miniature statues of ballerinas, and a powerful New Agey statuary collection with a stunned fellow watching birds circle the table where he was sitting. Like Mona, all were fashioned from mist outside the visual range of breathers and destined to evaporate in the first glow of the coming day.

I've always found a sort of peace at the art center. Specters who felt they still had something to say could keep working here. As though a roomful of lilies wasn't sufficient punctuation to end their monologue with the universe. But more importantly, it was clear proof that someone, some thing, or some force was in charge of the astral plane. There was order here, scales were balanced.

On the downside, these works lasted only a couple hours, were visible only to spooks and had the transparency of the mist. But, the spectral artists could move faster than hummingbirds on diet pills and they'd found a way to add color to their creations. So, like I said, it all balanced out.

I paused to watch an artist work on a giant misty canvas recording tonight's battle of Libby Hill. It was thrilling to see the event through a professional's eyes, although I don't recall horses writhing in agony on the ground, or white linen shirts streaked with blood or cannon balls exploding over the troops like grotesque blossoms.

During the course of the minute and a half I watched, the artist added a giant raven that trod around the side of the hill with various body parts dripping from its beak. Then the artist drifted back, studied the canvas, shook his head and painted over the raven with a highly detailed rendition of corsairs racing up the James River, sails flapping in the wind, muzzle-loaders being brought to bear on the defenders on the hill. (*Note to self: Go back to my earlier account of the battle and add the boats. I guess I was so engrossed in my own drama that I missed the fleet.*) By the time I wandered away, he was putting the raven back into the picture.

"How come you guys don't work inside?" I asked the artist.

With the sad smile of one who was now being misunderstood in his second life, he said, "The darkness is so much better out here."

"Ah, 'natch."

The corridors and display rooms of the arts center weren't the most comfortable place for a spook to be, owing to the security lights, but if you kept moving and suppressed any urge to stand around scratching every last inch of your body, it was okay.

In fact, the place was packed, testament to the determination of spooks to make the most of their afterlives. Or perhaps it was evidence of a misunderstanding common among decedents that since the arts are supposed to be the higher pleasures in life, then the arts should take more of their time since they're in a higher life.

I was startled by a familiar figure inside. And I use the word *figure* in a loose, shapeless sense. Dressed in sturdy but functional shoes, a sensible dress that came midway between ankle and knee, and a small black hat inspired by the uniform of a small eastern European fire department was the chairspook of the St. Sears group, Rosetta.

"Well, I say, Ralph, this is a fair treat." Rosetta, with distance from the low-lifes in Specters Anonymous, had taken on a faint British accent.

"What can I say?" I tried a sheepish smile that had *lamb* written all over it. "I got tired of embarrassing myself. I mean, am I the only one who doesn't know the difference between a collage and collards? Perhaps you have illustrations of both."

In a moment of uncertainty, Rosetta glanced quickly down several aisles, and I knew she was trying to remember where she'd seen a still life with the appropriate vegetable.

"You're pulling my leg," she said. "As it were."

"As I'd like it to be."

Suddenly, the old girl had steel in her gabardines. "One funeral wasn't enough for you, Ralph?"

I can't remember when a talk with Rosetta had been so much fun, but I was on a mission and I couldn't risk losing her cooperation.

"I was hoping," I said, penitentially, "to find information about a local artist. Name of Letitia Sanderling. She was big in ceramics in the late-1900s."

"As luck would have it, I believe I'm the only volunteer here tonight who knows anything about that artist. But as your misfortune would have it, I can't think of a single reason to be helpful."

"I'm trying to get a couple spooks into Specters Anonymous. They're being kept from coming, and it has something to do with this Letitia lady."

I've never known a spook in recovery who was unwilling to help someone on the path to transcendence. Rosetta was no exception, although it was a point of honor for her to make clear that her cooperation came despite — not because — I was the one asking.

"Actually, I've had a long interest in the case of Ms. Sanderling," Rosetta said as she led me around a crowd of rebel soldiers transfixed by the marble statue of a woman frozen in the exact moment her clothes were slipping from every relevant curve, limb and naughty bit.

"Oh?" I said, innocently.

Over her shoulder, Rosetta said, "I was hoping she might come here some night, Richmond being her home. And Letitia, in all likelihood, being dead."

I remembered the newspaper article. "She went missing. Her body was never found."

Rosetta's left eyebrow arched two degrees in amazement that I'd done any homework.

"At the end of her life, she fell under the influence of her lawyer and business manager, R. Everette Johnston, just as her work was gaining wider recognition. Some say he was embezzling from her, others say they had become intimate." Rosetta shot me a look that practically begged me not to ask what she meant by *intimate*.

Much as I enjoy watching Rosetta wriggle, sunrise was coming and I knew I wasn't going to get any rest if I didn't make some progress.

"Let me guess," I said. "R. Everett Johnston was investigated, but nothing against him was ever found. He washed his hands of Letitia Sanderling and went on to live a long and wealthy life."

"Not quite. Which is to say, you're right in all details but one."

I could see it hurt Rosetta to admit that I wasn't a total screw-up. I gave her a Mona Lisa smile, thought better of it, then gave her the Mona Lisa smile that Leonardo first painted.

"The attorney didn't, as you say, *wash his hands* of the missing artist. He announced Letitia had been secretly exploring new avenues in her work. Society was atwitter."

"So, R. Everette unveils the artwork. Letitia is proclaimed a genius. And he dies a wealthy man."

"No, not at all." Rosetta's expression was baffled until she remembered, I'm sure, that I actually was a screw-up. The old formality settled on her shoulders like an emperor's cape.

"Letitia's so-called *new direction in ceramics* was vulgar and childish. Her reputation never recovered. And I have no information about her counselor's estate at the time of his demise. I can't imagine that it amounted to much."

"Ah," I said. "That makes everything clear."

I drifted to the door, paused and turned back. "Just one other thing."

"Yes." Rosetta straightened so quickly I swear I heard her spine twang.

"When you said the artist and her lawyer were *intimate*, exactly what did you mean?"

Twenty-One

CHAPTER

One of the traditions at the arts center is the pre-sunup exhibition. After all, it's tough to store art made from mist, although I've heard of a spook who was using Cubism and new math to shake the foundations of modern sculpture. He found a way to get one of his nightly creations into the meat freezer at the Safeway grocery store. Sixteen hours later, when he went back to touch up his afterlife's masterpiece, it looked like an early Picasso, assuming Picasso worked in beef.

So, in the hour before sunlight drove Richmond's spooks back into the shadows, the artists, art-aficionados and Confederate soldiers looking for representations of the nude female form wandered among the pieces, accompanied by a few deceased critics who were attracted to the idea of digging their own holes deeper.

Men in ghostly gray were hooting and whistling in front of the Mona Lisa.

"Come on, old girl. How's about stepping out with Jared and me? There's still some life left in us. We'll show you a good time."

Mona looked at her artist-creator with soulful eyes that quite overshadowed the impact of Leonardo's cryptic smile. The artist shook his head. Mona shrugged, then waved. And the rebs turned away.

"I told you not to set your sights on that one, Jared. She wasn't what I'd call a woman of substance."

Mona Lisa frowned. Enigma-wise, that reaction wasn't as mysterious as her smile.

I dithered for a moment about going back to my regular bucket in Petey's house or to Randall's Inn of Spiritual Enlightenment, Alternative Recovery and Egomania.

Or to Margie's. I'd never spent the day *with* — that is to say, *in* — or better yet, *at* — Margie's. Physical intimacy isn't in the cards for specters, but isn't there something highly intimate about being around someone when your ectoplasm dematerializes for a few hours into its original, liquid state?

Was Margie ready for that? Was I?

(*Note to self: Next time I see Rosetta, ask her again for her definition of* intimacy. *I'll bet it has something to do with sharing the same wine glass.*)

(*Additional note to self: Ask Hank if he was serious when he said the reason we don't find virgins in the hereafter is because they've all been recruited for the welcoming committee in the Moslem zone.*)

It had been many nights since I watched an episode of *The Honeymooners* in Margie's back room. That silly, antiquated old sitcom was the only clue I had into my P.D. phase (that's *pre-decedence* for those who still think having rain blow into your face is neat). I can't move on with my transcendence until I deal with something that wasn't right with my first life.

Unfortunately, despite all evidence to the contrary, I am putty when duty calls. And my first responsibility was to my sponsor Cal, who was being pulled apart — literally, paranormally and ectoplasmicly — by Brother Randall and his tough, reject-everything-of-the-physical-world philosophy.

And to Gilda, who was playing a potentially dangerous game with his Uberness.

I hitched my astral trousers a little higher, gave Mona a wink and headed back to the warehouse behind the train station.

The sleeping quarters in Randall's compound stretched for miles of gloomy corridors within a narrow building that a breather could walk around in two or three minutes.

Shadows and fog mixed together to form the walls in a now-you-see-me-now-you-don't way that made them eerie even to me. And I helped make *boo* a word that can strike terror into the hearts of small children in darkened bedrooms and teenagers in crowded movie theaters.

I found the ceramic containers holding Hank, Gwendolyn and Cal next to each other in a dim hallway. Cal was restless, I could tell. He was probably as conflicted as the other Cal. I wondered if *conflicted* might be too apt a word. Maybe the only way to reunite the two halves of my best friend is by an old-fashioned bit of mayhem that leaves only one spook hovering at the end of the contest. And I would be left to spend hereafter with a buddy who was only half of his original self.

Gilda was in another dimly-lit corridor where, as near as I could tell, none of the adjacent pots were occupied. Post-mortality has got to be tough for a Goth. How do you express yourself, how do you prove you're a distinctive individual when everyone around you, left to his own devices, would have pasty skin, dark clothing and purple fingernails, too?

To be different you'd have to be sunshine and crinoline and good cheer. Which made me think of Darleen. And the blue-eyed tour leader for the spooks from Cincinnati. Who must be somewhere along these dark and empty hallways.

Wouldn't it be just neighborly to find out where little Blue-Eyes had her bucket? Maybe she hadn't sacked out yet for the day and would be interested in a stroll around the mausoleum.

A piece of paper sailed beneath my nose, followed by the snap of a clipboard that was barely under the control of the camp's secretary, Mrs. Pellywanger. She hove into view at an intersection, and I thought of the Flying Dutchman.

"There you are!" she said, spinning in my direction. "Why aren't you in your assigned pot? I've been looking for you half the night."

"This is the first I've heard of any assignment. I'd be happy to go there if you can tell me where it is."

"Oh, this is most distressing," Mrs. Pelly said. "Nothing goes where it should, stays where it should, or even cares that it should."

"That's a little harsh, ma'am. Like I said, no one told me about going to specific pots."

Mrs. Pelly giggled and, despite her sturdy sandals and the cloak made from fabric only marginally less in tensile strength than steel wool, managed to sound girlish.

"Not you." She flipped her wrist in my direction. "No, no, no. I was talking to my paperwork. I swear it sometimes behaves as though it has a mind of its own and I'm simply getting in its way."

She flapped the clipboard in my direction to offer the opportunity for confirmation, and I noticed a spook compressed into the size of a paperclip and wedged into the middle of the stack. He was yanking out papers and sending them drifting into the night.

Catching my eye, he tipped his hat. It had *Go Ohio* stenciled on the brim.

"Well, I'm glad you're here and alright," Mrs. Pelly said as her sandals took her back into the mist. "Have a good rest."

Something told me to keep my mouth shut, but I've never been good at listening to other people, so why should I treat myself any differently?

"Did you have something you wanted to tell me?" I called.

"Oh, my. Yes, I have a message." She looked at me with great earnestness. "I'm not bothered by being around all you dead people, night and day, but I worry about being here and being addled. Sounds like over-doing it a bit, doesn't it? And if I'm in happily-ever-after with only part of my original recipe, does this mean the other part of my mind is wandering out by itself in the sunshine? Without supervision?"

If you take the bait around Mrs. Pelly, you might end up drowning in the minnow bucket.

"You said something about a message."

"Brother Randall wonders if you might see him before calling it a night."

"Is that what he said?"

"That's the gist of it.""Would you care to give me the unedited version?"

"Oh, dear me, no." Her ashen features took on a kittenish blush. "Besides, I don't do well with thunderbolts and lightning."

"Then lead on."

We went at a breather's pace for less than thirty seconds, crossed a few intersections of corridors and took three or four turns. Then Mrs. Pelly stopped in the hall and gestured to a spot of wall no different from any other.

"What do I do now?" I asked.

"Click your heels three times, wiggle your nose and walk inside."

"Is the clicking and wiggling really necessary?"

"Only to most spooks."

I stepped through the wall with clickless, wiggleless self-assurance.

Randall was floating above a three-legged wooden stool and staring at the opposite wall, which put his back toward me. I saw in an alcove the same garishly inept ceramic pot I'd nearly slipped into earlier. If the room — a sort of mini-cavern, actually — had any other furniture, I couldn't tell, for a cloud of fog filled the chamber. I twirled my finger in front of my face, and eddies and ripples spread through the gloom.

Neato. A bit of repossessed property that wanted to play.

"What do you have for me, Ralph?" His Uberness swung around on his stool. "Have you carried out your mission?"

"Most definitely, sire." I snapped a salute and hoped I could buy some time to remember exactly what my assignment was.

"Of course, you have." Randall was as smooth as the hinge on a casket. "I know you have."

If I had any starch in my collar, it would have picked up its things and left by now. Had this creep or his minions been following me all night? Had I said or done anything that I was a few seconds from regretting?

"I tried to keep as normal a schedule as possible," I said, "so as not to arouse suspicion."

The fog, so playful a few moments ago, took on a dark, ominous tint. Things were moving in that gray darkness, small, worrying things. Things that can go anywhere, things in numbers that could overwhelm an unwary spook.

"Go on," Randall said. "Don't let my pets concern you."

Pets?

I swallowed hard and told my imagination it was too late in the night to worry about those old tales about demons that feed upon spooks. Or that can crawl into a spook's ears, get disoriented and end up popping out through his nose. If everyone's lucky.

"I stole into the enemy camp, most wrathful one. I saw that the hillside where your valiant troops were forced away by those cowardly soldiers and that yellow-streaked bird — that hillside was unmanned, unspooked and unguarded."

"Delightful," Randall said.

"At least, that is what they would have us believe." I gave my eyebrows a meaningful arch. "Fortunately for the forces of goodness, right and plunder, I decided upon a seemingly innocent stroll through the neighborhood. I even went to the art museum. Do you want to guess what I found?"

"No. Tell me."

"A trap." I arched my eyebrows higher. How does anyone do this without giving his entire forehead a cramp?

"Devious." Randall's smile was so large some of the glow trickled up to his enameled hair. "I'm beginning to like them."

"Your graciousness is entirely too… gracious. But these demons are hiding in homes, under children's beds, inside kitty litter trays, in refrigerators and beer cans. I think I saw an entire light cavalry regiment lurking in the wine bottles in the storage room of a restaurant."

"Is nothing sacred?" Randall snarled.

Few people did indignation as well as Brother Randall, and at the suggestion that some former sunshiners had found lodging in containers of alcoholic beverages, the reverend worked himself up into new heights of indignation, coupled with righteousness and resolve and sprinkled with just the subtlest hint of frustration.

"They will pay!" Randall thundered.

"Cash, credit or debit?" I thundered back. "Oh, oh. I see what you mean. Gotcha, chief."

CHAPTER Twenty-Two

rother Randall *poofed* away in mid-thunderation, and I was surprised to realize that so grand a spectral presence didn't have a more dramatic way than *poof* to announce his departure for another point on the astral plane.

Mrs. Pellywanger took me down the corridors of ceramic sleeping jars. With a gesture toward a simple container, somehow managing not to lose a piece of paper in the process, Mrs. Pelly shambled away.

I drifted in the dim light of the hall and glared down at the thin-necked, pot-bellied concoction of baked clay. If I ever saw another piece of ceramics again, I might transmogrify myself into a sixteen-pound hammer and ring some bells.

"Oh, the bells, bells, bells, bells, bells, bells, bells," I whispered.

"Will you show a little respect for great literature?"

Edgar Allan Poe lay on his side and floated over the pots in the corridor. He had a piece of straw angled from the corner of his mouth and a harmonica in his hand. His hat was swept to a rakish angle at the side of his head. (*And what, since we're on the subject, is a rakish angle? Forty-five degrees? Ninety? A hundred and eighty? It's bad enough that we use clichés, but must they be so imprecise?*)

Edgar A- gave me a squinty look. "They shoot spies here, don't you know?"

"I'm not a spy. I'm just ——"

"A purveyor of bad information who's not clear about his loyalties."

"Look, I'm tired."

"Tired? You don't know tired." The poet shook some spectral saliva from his harmonica. "Tired was Cold Harbor, Chancellorsville, the Wilderness."

"Don't try that on me." I climbed into my pot. "When those battles were fought, you'd been dead fifteen years."

"My point exactly."

Eventually, I glided into the liquefaction that passes for sleep in the Great Beyond, borne on a whispered lullaby from outside my hardened chamber:

"Keeping time, time, time / In a sort of Runic rhyme, / To the throbbing of the bells — / Of the bells, bells, bells — / Of the bells, bells, bells — / To the sobbing of the bells."

Randall's International House of Darkness did such a bang-up job blotting out the sunshine that I stayed longer in my bucket than usual and didn't emerge until a strange sound intruded upon my peace. It seemed to be made up of a broomstick at work and the low rumble of distant thunder.

Gilda was wafting up and down the corridor when I poured myself out. She looked smaller and more vulnerable than I remembered.

"What's that noise?" I asked.

"The faithful are assembling for the first ritual of the night."

"Is it fun?"

She tried to wave away my question. "If we're not there, it'll look suspicious. Listen, there's not much time. You've got to know something."

"What's to know? You're not a zombie. Let's figure out a way to get Cal out of here. Then let's hit the astral highway. I hear this is the perfect season to visit Nepal."

Her face wasn't a pasty white, her fingernails weren't purple and her eyes weren't hidden under layers of mascara and eyeliner. She looked as normal as you could expect for anyone whose funeral was a misty memory.

"Listen, I spent the day outside Randall's bucket," she said. "I heard him in there. He was talking to someone."

Technically, more than one specter can share the same container for our day-time rest, although what happens when their ectoplasm resolidifies is a scenario too grizzly to consider. It's not done. And it's not done with special vigor by a Spiritist like Randall, who would regard a shared bucket as something suspiciously similar to friendliness.

"Do you know who was in there?" I asked. An idea unbecoming for a spirit on the path to transcendence came to me. "It wasn't a spook of the formerly female persuasion, was it?"

"*Formerly female.* I really hate it when you call us that."

"Is there something about yourself that you're not telling me? Something embarrassing and personal. Like a career as a mud-wrestler."

Gilda hovered in the dusky air, both hands planted on her hips; her eyes reminded me of the giant raven's.

"This is my point," she finally said. "We haven't even begun to scratch the surface here. There are entities here we can't trust that we don't even know about."

"Can you be more cryptic?"

"Certainly, but not right now." Gilda drifted closer, and from the way she looked at my shirt, I was sure I was seconds away from a thorough shaking. "Whoever was in Randall's bucket wasn't one of us."

"Not a spook?" One possibility leaped at me. "Mrs. Pellywanger!"

"I don't mean that." She squinched her nose in thought. I never noticed before that Gilda actually had a cute squinch. "I don't know what I mean. *That's easy for you to say*, Randall told his visitor a couple times. *You're not like us. You don't go through what we put up with.* Yet I'm sure it was a spook."

"Any chance it was a large black bird?"

When we emerged into the twilight, Randall's followers gathered on the cracked cement yard outside the building facing the train station. By now, most were wearing monk's robes with hoods pulled over their heads and sandals on their feet. The sound that had reached into my bucket and pulled me awake was dozens of ghostly feet sliding through the corridors.

Outside, no one spoke or gawked or fidgeted. I was going to stand out like a cactus in a prom bouquet.

Near the edge of the crowd closest to the warehouse was Cal. I made my way to the remnant of my sponsor.

"How about you and me checking out the goings-on at the diner?" I hoped the other Cal, what I'd come to think of as *my Cal,* was still there. "We'll be back by bucket-check. I promise."

"Are *they* going to be there? You know? People?"

According to my reading of the spook, Cal had just said a dirty word.

"No diner's going to stay in business waiting for the likes of you and me to pick up the bill. Even the mortuaries and cemeteries make us pay in advance."

"Yes," Cal whispered. "Now is the best time of our existence. We only have to take it one night at a time. But we must avoid Glow Bugs and the places they infest. Only by willing ourselves to be pure spirits, each a part of the essence of the universe, can we evolve into our true beings."

Cal looked at me with a weird shadow in his eyes. "You know where evolution ends, don't you?"

"In a fundamentalist preacher's pulpit?"

Cal shook his head. "In the shadows. We are all destined to join that great darkness stretching across the universe, the void that is most of everything that is."

"That's really super," I said. "I aspire to eat less sugar, be kinder to animals and finally learn to dance the polka."

Cal crossed his arms over his chest and gazed at the ground as he drifted away. For a spirit in two locations, he wasn't even as thick as the mist outside the art center last night, but he had the same fierce concentration I've come to expect of him as he studied the cracked, up-heaved concrete slabs.

The old Cal was here. Somewhere.

I glanced at Gilda. "How long do you think he'll last?"

"Give him five seconds. Then take another look."

I waited two seconds. When I turned back to Cal, three or four of Randall's spooks had gathered around him. Wearing brown monk's robes, they stepped to Cal, one by one, and gave him a manly embrace. Including a specter who was a former estrogen carrier. Cal kept his arms across his chest and his head down as each stepped back after an affirming hug.

A week ago, I would have said he was daring them to try something. Now, I'm not so sure. Was that shyness on my old sponsor's stony face? Fear? Apathy?

A hulking specter with the face of a bloodhound said to him, "If I don't see you again, my friend, may the shadows rise up to greet you."

"And the blackness welcome you as its own," replied Cal and the others in sing-song fashion.

Up until that moment, I was willing to give Brother Randall the benefit of the doubt and wish the old buzzard the best on his road to recovery. But whatever goodwill was in me turned into dust.

I realized I disliked Brother Randall with an intensity unbecoming for a spook who manages brave noises about traveling the path to transcendence, hated him for making Cal divided and insecure and unhappy. But mostly I hated him for making Cal small.

A ripple of energy passed through the spooks gathered on the bare concrete lot and, like toilet water finding an open drain, they flowed toward the clock tower of the train station.

Brother Randall hovered above the roof where Gwendolyn, Hank and I had hidden last night to scope out the place. The night was a velvet curtain in the background, setting off Randall's noble figure. He was in full glory and wore a robe that was partially Harry Potter, partially the last royal wedding at Westminster Cathedral. His slicked-down hair sparkled with the city's reflected light to create the eerie impression that a crown rested above that fatherly forehead.

His smile was full, but something about the eyes made me think of Moses returning from Mount Sinai to discover the chosen people at a toga party.

Randall spread his arms. A hush fell over his followers. "Last night, my brother and sister spirits who have been assembling for centuries at the corners of the earth were barred from joining us in this city."

The hush that fell on the crowd got deeper, and I was thinking again about that toilet bowl.

"Do you know why they were unable to join us?" Randall smiled down on the faithful. "Do you know who made them unable to join us?"

I looked at Gilda, but she was drifting away. All the spooks in the area were drifting away from me. I was becoming that cactus in the bouquet.

Did I mention that I was leading a scientific expedition to Tierra del Fuego to survey the fungus? Have I neglected to point out that I'm late for my flight?

"They didn't come because"— Randall had that smile that stayed on his face like a dead rat until, like a crack of thunder heralding the end of the world, he added —"WE FAILED THEM!"

The assembled spooks did a group-cringe. Gwendolyn and Hank made their way slowly toward me. I saw an unusual patch of darkness on Hank's shoulder.

"Look who the cat dragged in." Hank's pigtail bobbed with delight near Shade, who lay on Hank's shoulders.

Shade glanced at Cal and asked, "What's wrong with my buddy?"

"Too much religion," I said.

"Or too little," Shade said. The night air was giving the little fellow some spunk.

I sensed, more than saw or heard, a disquiet spread through the assembled masses. "Something's wrong," a spook whispered.

When I glanced up toward the clock tower, Randall was just where I had last seen him. And that was the problem. Arms outspread, mouth grimacing with the admission he'd been forced to make, shoulders slumped as though preparing to accept more blows from the forces of injustice, Randall hadn't moved.

Pregnant pauses I've heard of. This one could have come sliding down the chute of a beluga whale.

Twenty-Three
CHAPTER

Ever been in a car crash and felt time stretch out like a rubber band? You can't say anything or move a muscle but you're fully alert as you glide in slow-motion toward a tree on the edge of the road?

Watching Randall hover in the sky on the clock tower was exactly like that, but without the road or the car or the tree.

Even when he started talking again and time returned to its normal tick-tock, the car-crash image lingered, blotting out the paranormality around me. I couldn't hear his voice. Although I was staring at him, would I have noticed if he had jumped up and down like a chimpanzee?

Of course, that was the answer. Not the bit about the chimpanzee. But the crash. It felt like I was remembering something because I was. For only the second time in my afterlife, I'd actually dragged a major, significant, transcendence-altering memory through the Great Divide.

A less mature spook would have whooped. I grabbed Gwendolyn by the lapels and shook him until his eyes started to bulge.

"It was a crash. I can see it. I can even feel it. The long sideways slide that took forever. Just think of that. Ain't that something?" I slapped my hands, hopped around, pretended to exhale, and otherwise comported myself like one who never learned how to behave in public.

"Ssssshhhhhhh," came from several sides.

Gilda shot me a look. The corners of her eyes crinkled, the edges of her mouth tightened. Which was a Goth's version of somersaults across the concrete.

Gwendolyn dissolved in my grip (*poof*) and reappeared a safe five feet away, his eyes locked on Randall on the tower.

"The big finish," I chattered. "The final ticket stamp. The grand exit. I know it now. I know."

From out of nowhere, Hank appeared in front of me and thrust Gwendolyn's half-chewed cigar into my mouth. Thanks to my old buddy, never will I have to wonder what it would be like to have a handful of river bank mud jammed down my throat. I whipped that soggy turd from my mouth and spat, hacked and wiped my teeth, gums and tongue on my spectral sleeve. Venom was in my eyes (*I knew that because my vision went off-yellow*) as I glared holes in Hank. He wasn't going to get away with this: a moment of reckoning was coming and I wanted him to know so he had plenty of time to worry about it.

Cool as a spook who'd just stepped from the refrigerator at the morgue, Hank picked up the stogie, daintily blew away the dirt that wasn't on it, and offered it back to Gwendolyn.

"Two things," he said. "First, was this accident the big one? Or might it have happened some other day as a breather? Second, before you start cogitating about that, you better pay attention to what's happening here. Things are getting ugly."

He was right, of course, about what we call *rebooted memory*. A moment from sunshine days is just that — a single moment. And unless you're lucky enough to find a notarized written statement, you're not sure what you've got.

None too gently, Hank pinched my chin with his fingers and aimed my face toward Brother Randall.

"— fault is ours," Randall was saying. "Ours alone. We must atone — we WILL atone. This terrible defeat was a sign from the great Uber-Spirit. We have allowed ourselves to be tainted, corrupted and putrefied by physicality. We must purify ourselves."

Randall gazed upon his followers, then added: "We will talk more about this later. Please make this night one of reflection. Open yourselves to the Uber-Spirit."

He returned to the tattered warehouse as though gliding down a cable strung between the clock tower and the door of his headquarters. From the wave of *oo's* and *ah's* that spread through the spooks below him, you'd think no one had ever seen a specter in flight before.

I sought my old sponsor in the crowd.

"Cal," I said, "I've got to talk. Something happened a few minutes ago. I think it's important to my transcendence."

Cal waved me away. "I don't have the time. There's so much to do. We must be purified."

Because I was sure of only one place where I could lick my wounds in private, I left my friends at Brother Randall's Reformatory for Wayward Specters and headed east.

Petey had taken up her station in the dining room to the left of James William's chair as the family clinked and clattered their way through dinner. When the beagle saw me in the living room, she joined me by the sofa after giving her family a look that clearly said: *No one leaves until I say so. And I expect to be notified immediately if any little accidents happen.*

I stretched out on the floor and Petey lay down in front of me. We were practically brushing noses.

I hate to admit it, but Hank was probably on target. I didn't have any reason to believe the memory that'd just slipped into the hereafter was the last one I had in the sunshine. As a matter of fact, the longer I sloshed it around in my head — the ballet of a car turning slowly until its side was leading the way toward another car, whose driver turned, startled, mouth frozen in a shout that probably never left his lips, while the car I was in slid past him to the tree — the less certain I was that this memory involved the big finish.

Like my first real posthumous memory, which mostly involved the smells I associated with my grandmother, this one wasn't locked down to a specific time or event.

"Have you got any ideas, girl?" I asked Petey.

From her deep chocolate eyes came a warm flood of understanding. She moaned with compassion, lifted her head to glance over her shoulder at the family in the dining room, then settled her chin back on her paws.

"Yeah, you're right," I whispered. "We just gotta put one paw in front of the other and keep going. You have a family to supervise in the dining room. I've got to help some spooks through post-mortality."

Petey looked at me with her wide, soothing peepers. I wouldn't want to play poker with this dog. She could manage to shower me with all the understanding from two planes of existence but, at the same, let me know that the decision was mine and she wasn't going to agree or disagree with the course I picked.

The enormity of the job panicked me. "Thing is, which spook do I help first? There are hundreds of them at Brother Randall's. Is it fair for me to help Cal, just because he's my sponsor?"

Petey blinked. I've never known a creature — man, spook or canine — who could say more with the flutter of an eyelid.

"You're right, of course," I said. "Gilda, Hank and Gwendolyn can look after Cal right now. For that matter, Hank and Gwendolyn can also look after Gilda. If I try to save everyone, I can't save anyone. Just *one poor, still-suffering spook* at a time, that's what Cal always said. Though, maybe tonight, I can push it a little and try for two."

Petey pulled herself to her paws and gave her coat a good shake. She had a family at a dinner table who'd gone long enough without her guidance.

The neon sign in Carytown still said *Psychic Advisor*, but a piece of paper was now scotch-taped to the window below the glowing letters. I drifted closer to the bay window and read: *Alterations While You Wait*.

The waiting room wasn't entirely empty. I recognized three spooks who were hovering over the sofa from my Specters Anonymous meetings. They were pranksters who obviously hadn't learned that Margie wasn't like Madame Sophie or any of the other local psychics: Margie was the real deal, and they weren't going to cross her wires as easily as they could with Madame Sophie.

The only paying customer in the waiting room was a young man leafing through a magazine in his underwear.

Margie was in her consultation room, a pair of blue jeans stretched across the fish bowl in the center of the table. She looked up; a needle and thread were in her hand.

"Have you fixed that little problem?" she asked me.

"I'm working on it."

"I want results, Mister. Not promises."

"It's coming along." I almost added, *Keep your shirt on*, but under the circumstances, that remark seemed in bad taste even for me.

Then I realized she wasn't alone. Sitting opposite her, a steaming cup of tea in a gnarled hand, was Madame Sophie.

Soph looked squarely at me and said, "Good evening."

"Evening," I replied. I did a double-take, perhaps even a triple. Sophie was known for getting her signals straight a couple nights a year. I guess I was going to finally see what the old girl was like in her prime.

"Please, don't let me interfere with your business with Margie." Sophie used a grand gesture to indicate I could hover wherever I wanted.

"Thanks, I'll just be a minute."

"As you wish," Sophie said.

Had I been too rough on the old fraud? Maybe Sophie was alright. At least, when the wind was from the southwest, the temperature was mild with no overcast, and Soph hadn't begun her quality control checks of the apricot brandy.

"Sophie and I were talking about the possibility of opening a joint practice," Margie said. There was a smile on her lips but her eyes were what you'd expect for a guard working alone on the nightshift in the state penitentiary's wing for homicidal maniacs.

"It would be fun to have some companionship," Margie added, with genial anxiety. "And having a colleague would mean a financial cushion for the bad nights and leveling out the workload when we're packing them in."

Sophie waved her hand and three dozen bracelets on her bony wrist went clattering and clinking.

"I hope you don't find that offensive?" Sophie asked me. "I refer to the phrase *packing them in?*"

I didn't know whether to be agreeable or irked that Soph thought the world had a shortage of political correctness.

"No," I said. "That's fine."

"Good. I'm glad," Sophie answered.

By now, Margie's eyes had gone from the size of saucers, outgrew the dimensions of plates and passed into platter territory.

"Look," Margie told me. "This is a bad time. Why don't you stop by later? I'd love to have a little chat. But I don't want to be rude to my other guest."

"Please, please, children, not on my account." Sophie gripped the edge of the table and pulled herself to her feet. Given her notion of the vertical, I think she'd already begun her quality control work for the distillery.

"I'm going," I said. "Just passing through."

"No, I won't hear it," Soph said.

"While you're here," I told Sophie, "perhaps I could ask you a question or two about Letitia Sanderling."

"I will give you a ring tomorrow, dear, after we've all had our beauty rest," Sophie said to Margie. Then turning to me she added, "It's been very nice meeting you."

"Thirty seconds. Is that too much?" I asked.

"Wonderful, wonderful," Sophie replied.

I locked eyes on Margie; my favorite psychic advisor was trying to hide in the pants she was mending. She was seconds from dropping her head in the fish bowl that served as her environmentally conscious crystal ball.

"Say it ain't so, Marg," I said.

"Let me explain," she pleaded.

I zipped next to Madame Sophie as she stomped her way through the corridor from Margie's waiting room. I nestled my chin on her shoulder. And I said:

"BOO!"

Twenty-Four

CHAPTER

s a member of the spectral *hoi polloi*, I don't hold myself as being so special that I will never use the *B*-word. Sometimes I just gotta get it out of my system. In this case, the three spooks loitering around Margie's waiting room haven't been seen since I ran that little auditory check on Madame Sophie. There have been reports, which I'm not interested in enough to confirm, that around the time of that minor blow-up, Specters Anonymous acquired its first chapter on a lesser moon of Uranus. And Petey, who was several miles away on Libby Hill, started howling in concert with most of Richmond's canine population.

Margie had her nose pressed against her latest client's blue jeans when I returned to her consulting room.

"Are you really going into business with that fraud?" I asked her.

"Yep."

If embarrassment could be harnessed to a good speaker system, Margie could clear Richmond of the rest of its post-mortal population, most of its breathers, all of its dogs and cats, and a fair percentage of its rats and cockroaches.

I tried to slink into a chair. "Times are tough, huh? Maybe we can put our heads together and come up with something."

"It's not that," she said. "Which isn't to say that it's not a factor. It is, but at the same time it's not. Am I being clear?"

"Perfectly." Actually, I was relieved she wasn't looking anymore like a water-logged puppy. Or like Cal. And, as with a puppy and with Cal, there wasn't much for me to do under the circumstances. I had to fold my hands on the table and wait for them to shake themselves dry.

"I get so lonely," she finally said. "I spend twenty hours a day by myself in these rooms, telling myself I have to be here in case a customer comes. The other four hours — if I'm lucky — I spend with people who are so hurt and confused they barely notice me. And, a lot of times, those people's dead loved ones are floating around my ears, trying to apologize for their selfishness and heartlessness."

She put down her sewing and pinned me with a look that reminded me she was a genuine psychic. "But do you know what's the worst thing I hear?"

I'm not sure I wanted to know this, but I had to say, "What?"

"The ones who aren't there. Not when they were walking the earth, not when they're in your dimension. Not even when they're standing in your world and trying to talk to loved ones in mine. They're simply not there."

"Yeah, I hate it when that happens."

So when Margie said she only had a couple minutes left to repair her customer's jeans and would I be interested in watching an episode or two of *The Honeymooners*, I couldn't say I was supposed to be somewhere else.

In her back room, she put on a DVD from the show's first season. Margie was so relaxed and chattered so freely and I was feeling so good to be around her when she wasn't gritting her teeth, that I didn't have the heart to tell her I really had stuff to do.

The episode that came up was about Ralph, played by comedian Jackie Gleason, getting a botched message from his doctor that let him think he was dying. My fictional fifties namesake was crushed that he didn't have anything to leave his wife, so he decided to let a newspaper buy the exclusive tale of a dying man.

The episode made me uncomfortable. It was hitting close to home, but I couldn't figure why.

"I guess you don't need another reminder of death," was Margie's explanation after I explained my reaction.

"That's like telling a fish you don't want to bore him by talking about water. What else is there to talk about?"

Margie was starting to droop, so I told her I still had a long night ahead of me. Truer words were never more accidentally spoken. We were all smiles when she turned off her neon sign. I zipped through the front door and once out of sight, looped around and headed for the upper floor of her building.

Whiner and Sniveler were having an argument inside the world's ugliest ashtray when I arrived, and the closest I could come to figuring out the topic was Whiner's remark about Sniveler's failure to help *picking up around the place*. That opened a topic I didn't want to explore too closely.

"Yeeeeesssssshhhhh?" Sniveler asked before I could open my mouth.

"Sorry, guys," I replied. "Didn't mean to sneak up on you."

"Why should anyone try to sneak up on us?" Sniveler said. "We're only spooks who've been stuck here — wherever *here* is — and maybe we'd appreciate a little surprise. Not that we want to sound demanding or unappreciative to a godhead."

"Besides, Your Deityness," Whiner added, "you couldn't sneak up on us if you tried. An ant couldn't do it. Nor a gnat. Not even a floating smidgen of dust."

"Why's that?"

"You've heard about people who lose one sense, and have some other sense get magnified? Well, take a good look at us. Ask yourself: Exactly what do these spooks do to kill time?"

"You could meditate."

"What?" Whiner answered. "Every time I try that stuff I fall asleep. I hope I'm not offending your all-knowing self, Great Ralph, but falling asleep isn't something that, under my current circumstances, I need a lot of help doing."

That put me in mind of the TV show — poor Ralph Kramden with dark circles under his eyes that Gilda, in her Goth period, would have envied. Tearing himself apart because he didn't see the simple obvious step that was right in front of him. In Ralph Kramden's case, it was calling his doctor and finding out there was a misdiagnosis.

What was there about Whiner and Sniveler that was so obvious that I couldn't see it?

"When your ashtray starts rattling and quaking," I said, "you're not the ones doing the rattling and quaking, right?"

"This is a test," Whiner said. "You are testing our worthiness."

"Exactly. Now answer the question: Are you making your ashtray move?"

"Do I wish," Sniveler said. "Leave it to me, and I'd knock this piece of dried clay into a gazillion pieces."

"So, when the ashtray shakes —"

"Excuse me, Your All Knowingness," Whiner added, "but the ashtray never shakes. Something else in the room is shaking. If it weren't, we'd be the first to know."

"*Second* to know," Sniveler said. "The Great God Ralph would be the first."

"Hmmm. And whenever whatever rattles, is anything else happening? Any voices? Noises? Any particular time of day or night?"

"We're chronologically challenged," Whiner said, "seeing as how we can't tell day from night. But judging by the way it's so quiet outside, it must be night."

"Was anything special going on?" I asked. "Thunderstorms or ambulance sirens in the street or wind brushing against the roof?"

"Can't say there was," Whiner said.

"How are we doing, Your Ralphness? Are we proving ourselves to be true followers of your inestimable teachings?" Sniveler added, restless after two minutes without groveling to someone.

"You're breaking all records," I assured them. "Let me think. Is there talking in the street? People passing by? College kids goofing around? Any of that going on that might trigger these"— I suddenly realized I was trying to diagnose the problems of a talking ashtray and fought against the impulse to hang my head in shame and float back to Petey and my bucket on Libby Hill —"these spasms in your world?"

"Noises on the street? Can't say that applies. It being night and all, things are pretty quiet out there. What do you say?"

Quickly, Sniveler said, "I defer to you, boss. Eagle eye and rabbit ears. Talking purely about acuity, you understand. Size doesn't factor."

"Roger," Whiner said.

I also understood that spooks like me who believe they're receiving personal messages from sixty-year-old sitcoms are sometimes left outside on a hot July afternoon.

"No voices at all, huh?" I added.

"Well, no," Whiner said.

"I wouldn't go so far as to say *no voices*."

"But our divineness clearly made the word a plural," Whiner said. "I heard the *s*."

"And your point is —" Sniveler was showing a little spunk.

"The question as posed, with a big fat *s* sitting at the end of that noun, would require a definite, *No*. We have not heard voices."

There was a point here. Somewhere. I squinted at the ashtray and brought my head closer.

"You're saying the answer is *No*," I said, "if the question is about voices. Emphasis upon the plural."

"I see why he got the job of running the universe," Whiner said.

"Don't rush him. He's under a lot of pressure."

I squeezed my eyelids shut. "That means." Long pause, trying to find the thread of sanity in the clutter of words. "That means the answer is *Yes* if the question is about —"

"A single voice!" Sniveler whooped with glee. "Yes, sir, there's no Ralph like our Ralph. Next to our Ralph, all the other morons are idiots."

I clenched the side of the shelf. If I weren't a non-corporeal being whose fingers passed through the metal plate as though it were mashed potatoes, I would have left dents there.

"You're telling me that when this rattling starts, a single voice is talking?"

"Well, since you put it that way," Whiner said reluctantly. "Yes."

"Is it the same voice?"

"The same as what?" Sniveler was showing more spunk than was healthy for him.

"The same voice that always speaks whenever that rattling happens."

"Oh, that voice." Sniveler was back to his own fawning self. "Yes, it's always that very same voice."

If my lower lip wasn't an astral substance, I believe I would have bitten it off right then. My eyes lost their focus: put that down to the steam rising from my ectoplasm.

"I suppose you're going to say that you didn't tell me about the voice because I didn't ask."

"Gosh," Sniveler replied. "We can't get anything past you, Your Keenness."

My conversation with Whiner and Sniveler soon shrank into a series of one-syllable answers delivered in increasingly soft tones by the two spooks. With practically anyone else, I'd have thought they were sulking or finally embarrassed by misleading me for precious days.

Anyone trapped in a repulsive contraption of fire-dried clay, however, was beyond mere humiliation. Something else was going on, and the most meaningful explanation came when Whiner admitted that "someone here was making me nervous" in a confidential whisper that led me to believe he wasn't talking about me or Sniveler.

Was the owner of the mysterious voice lurking somewhere amid the boxes of legal documents and shelves of kindergarten-grade ceramic pieces? I could hear Whiner and Sniveler growing smaller by the question, until, after Sniveler had volunteered that he thought the voice came from a spook of the formerly male inclination, I decided I was verging on cruelty to continue to press them.

Let them slink away to wherever they found refuge.

"Thanks for your help, guys. I'll check in on you later."

As I backed away from the shelf and prepared for a rapid exit to Church Hill, Whiner asked, "Did we mention the roundness? I don't think we did."

"The round what?"

"The round words. When that voice comes to us, all the words are round."

"What do you mean?"

I could hear Whiner and Sniveler whisper earnestly between each other, but neither answered my question.

Twenty-Five

Since it was a while before the start of my regular meeting — if, that is, there would ever be a regular meeting, what with so many of my friends in recovery now committed to Brother Randall's path to transcendence — I went to one of the favorite diners for the St. Sears group near the campus. I saw Rosetta and Darleen sharing a corner booth in the back with a couple breathers. I nodded, then slid into a booth near the front to be alone.

By *alone*, I wasn't counting the sunshiners who were sharing an apple pie *a la mode* while they sipped iced tea and talked with the nonchalance of Frenchmen about the latest assignments in their philosophy course.

Round words. What made a word round? What made any sound round? I wasn't willing to dismiss Whiner's last comment as the ravings of a haunted mind. Surely, I'd heard sounds that were round before. It's called music. But talking?

Back and forth across the table top, the intellectuals traded arch references like finalists at Wimbledon, and I could hear the syllables snap with well-studied precision.

"… from *Kant*…"

"… his *categorical* im*per*ative…"

151

"I can *posit* that…"

Those words were crisp, sharp. What words were round?

"Bowl," I said. "Boooooowwwllll."

Then: "Rrrrooooooll."

And finally: "Hooooooollllle."

I sat back, pleased with myself, having proved to the doubting masses — who were out there somewhere — that words could definitely have curved edges.

"Rigmarole." Unless I was sorely out of touch, this last suggestion didn't come from me, followed quickly by: "Casserole. Tadpole."

I looked over my shoulder for the voice. Nothing. When I turned back to the two philosophers, Edgar Allan Poe had joined them on the bench on the other side of the table.

"If we had a genuinely hedonistic civilization," Poe said, "I should be able to think of four or five couplets that end with *casserole*. If we were more kindly toward nature, I could manage at least two sonnets that rhyme *tadpole*. And if we were more frivolous, we'd have put *rigmarole* to better employment, rhyme-wise."

"You're kidding."

"I'm sure I wouldn't know."

Edgar A- floated up through the table and was halfway to the ceiling before I lunged for his feet. His foot dissolved into nothingness as my spectral fingers closed upon the remnants of his toes.

"Where do I find round words?" I asked.

For the first time in our brief relationship, I caught the great spook's curiosity. Or perhaps it was just an ectoplasmic gas bubble that made his mouth twist that way while his eyes squinted.

"I presume you've tried looking upon the surface of a child's ball."

This, I realized, wasn't going to come easily or cheaply. I shook my head.

"Perhaps a printer's shop. I understand they can do amazing things these days with typography."

"Round words," I said, staring firmly at him. "I want a serious answer, and I want it now."

"Oh, really." Poe glanced out the store's front window, where a bird's foot with claws the size of telephone poles descended from the night, followed by fluff from an ebony feather that covered three cars.

I managed to put a little ice into my voice. "I can get to you before your friend can get to me."

Poe measured the distance between us. As a student, I've heard, he was good in math, and from the nervous creases that sprang to his wide forehead, he still remembered some of those lessons.

He said, "Leave me unmolested, and I shall give you the correct answer."

I don't know why I took the word of a former drunk, recovering drug addict, occasional madman and — I shudder to think the words — long-time literary critic. Maybe I'm just a sucker for dead poets who like dragging the tails of their black coats through hot fudge.

Pointedly, I leaned back and crossed my arms. "And what might that be?"

"You will find your round words"— he made a bold study of my face, searching, I was sure, to see if I could stand the truth —"on the lips of those who use round words when they speak."

(*Note to self: Next time I feel the urge to bandy words about, remember to play with someone besides a former professional word-bandyier.*)

Poe left, and while I can't honestly say that things were beginning to fall into place, I think they were starting to lean in a helpful direction.

I waved to Rosetta and Darleen as I left the diner, and in two flicks of a bat's toe, I was back on Libby Hill near the Confederate memorial under a clear nighttime sky. The wind rising from the river carried scents of the sea, of seaweed and water-logged timbers. The sounds of the city, now falling asleep, were like a dreamer's low moan.

The colonel was at his post, walking the lonely perimeters of the hill.

"Still quiet?" I asked.

"Yes. Much obliged for making that happen."

"Me?"

"I heard about your little talk with the enemy commander." The barest crinkle of amusement touched the corner of the old vet's eyes. "Troops hiding out in basements, filling homes from the ceiling to the floors, stacked up like firewood in pantries."

"Well, even spooks have their moments."

He nodded in reply. For a taciturn soldier from the days when combat meant looking a man in the eye as you sent him beyond the Great Divide, a nod was high praise. And for it to come so quickly after my talk with Brother Randall —

"Wait a minute. How come you know what I said to him. He and I were the only ones in that room."

"Apparently not," the colonel replied.

I knew it might cost me the respect of a spook I was coming to admire, but I pressed him for a while. Trying to wheedle, charm and flimflam him out of a little information that would let me know how — and from whom — he received his intelligence.

Other than a half-hearted, "Not all soldiers wear uniforms," I wasn't able to get him to say more. In a rare spasm of common sense, I decided not to try threatening him.

I scanned the heavy shadows by the river. "You think they'll come tonight?"

"They're up to something over there." He looked to the clock tower by the railway station where Randall had his headquarters. "I suspect we'll hear from them tonight. Maybe not the big show, but something."

I took a last look from the hilltop. The James River glinted silver beneath a quarter-moon. In the wooded east, the lights of scattered homes gave the impression of campfires burning.

"What would you say if I asked you about round words?"

"Wouldn't say nothing."

"Why?"

"Only an idiot, drunk or a child would ask a question like that. And I stand aside from discussions with them."

"I agree entirely," I said. "Did I happen to mention I'm five years old?"

"'Twarn't necessary."

Although it was still early for my meeting, I wandered over to the church basement that the St. Sears group called home.

A bulb burning inside the meeting room cast a perfect square of light on the sidewalk below the window. I could see Fast Eddie walking slowly between the gray metal chairs inside as a cloud of tiny black dots floated in front of his face.

Fast Eddie had been a Tosser early in his recovery, and while he'd abandoned his rock-chucking ways, he still enjoyed tapping into his powers of levitation to sprinkle the meeting room with coffee beans. He once told me the smell of coffee comforted a lot of our specters, especially the newbies, who were used to floating on a sea of coffee during the 12-step meetings of their first lives.

Even though he knew I was aware of this quaint chore, which Brother Randall would doubtless condemn as dangerous, even heretical, I waited outside until Fast Eddie was done. He meant well; there was no sense making him uncomfortable.

The last bean was still rolling under a chair and I was starting through the closed door when Fast Eddie darted outside.

"Sorry, kid," he said and scooted past, not able to meet my eye.

He didn't need to say more. Silence was easier on me, too. Silence gave me the room to pretend that I didn't know he was moving stakes to Brother Randall's operation.

So long as one spook is sitting in a basement room, all the breathers who reach their expiration dates and wander into Specters Anonymous some night will have hope.

That was Cal's way of putting it. I remembered that phrase for its quiet wisdom and authority. I also remember Cal having to go to the back of the diner and lie down after making that little speech because so many words hadn't passed his lips in a single burst for decades.

The clock on the wall showed nearly ten minutes before the start of the nightly meeting, and I was feeling a kinship with the old rebel soldier on the hill. We were two lonely pickets, standing guard in the night. The colonel to warn if danger approached, me for the spooks who realize that getting a ride in a hearse to your own personal underground bunker still doesn't make us safe from ourselves.

I watched each twitch of the clock's second hand. Rosetta and Darleen came inside, then, after a discreet gap, a couple spooks still shaky from their last exposure to sunlight, a few old-timers who were part of the St. Sears irregulars, then, last but certainly not least, Cal. My Cal, minus the Cal who hung out with Brother Randall.

Rosetta called the meeting to order and asked if anyone was within their first thirty years of recovery. Cal raised a hand.

If I had a physical tongue, it would have been three-quarters of the way to my knees. Rosetta looked as though she'd *poof* away at any moment. Darleen leaned forward in her chair. Darleen was prepared to *poof* into another dimension if the language here got ugly.

"Technically, I haven't had a stumblie," Cal said. "But only technically. If I'd seen a grow-light on my way over here, I... I don't know what I would have done."

Cal looked down at his hands. Like he was taking their measure, like he wasn't sure what they were willing to do for him, for good or ill.

Rosetta said, softly, "Why don't you lead the meeting, Cal?"

Cal didn't say anything for quite a while and when he looked up, he was staring at the newbies. Newbies always got him focused.

"If that's the case," he said, "I'd like to open with the Transcendence Prayer."

Rosetta nodded. As though anyone needed permission to recite the prayer that's one of the few things that all members of Specters Anonymous agree upon, making allowances, of course, for the various minorities who feel it goes too far toward Spiritism, not far enough, misses the point or could be improved by a strong rewrite.

"Uber-Spirit ——" Cal began.

Gilda's image flashed across my mind and I said a quick little prayer that whatever entity held the ownership papers for ever-after would look carefully after her.

"Uber-Spirit," the others repeated. "Help me to do the things I can do, to stop trying to do the things I cannot do, and to give me a slap upside the head to quit analyzing the previous requests."

When we finished, I felt better. Cal spent more time looking at the newbies than his hands as he talked — a good sign — telling them about the way he envied the Spiritists, about whether it was honesty, pride or fear that kept him from joining them, about his wish that he could find some way to slip off the leash of reason and fly through the night air with them, trusting his feelings, being a part of the great universe where physicality and paranormality weren't two sides of the same coin.

"I wonder if our first lives and our second ones might be even closer than that," Rosetta said, showing a rare appreciation for subtlety. "Sometimes I think if I can only step to one side quick enough, I'd find myself back in the material world. And I'm sure, when I was a proper breather, I wondered about doing a quick sidestep that would have brought me to the hereafter."

The new comers, I could tell, were fired up by the freshness of these thoughts. The first spooks you hear talk about the humdrum realities of the afterlife always sound like the world's greatest thinkers.

By the time the meeting broke up, Cal was surrounded by newbies. Darleen had a wistful glimmer in her eye, and I heard Rosetta talking softly to her.

Darleen might be the next one of the old group to find her way into Brother Randall's influence. But Rosetta and Cal were solid. So long as Cal — or, at least, what remained of him — was working with newcomers, he'd be okay.

Twenty-Six CHAPTER

I floated through the door into the night air. Cal, I was sure, would be holding a meeting-after-the-meeting in the River City Diner for the newbies, and I knew I'd be welcome, but Cal would be okay doing the thing he did best — helping the poor, recovering spook – and I had other ectoplasm to fry.

I felt better than I had in a while. Hopeful. *We don't need to save every spook in the cemetery*, Cal liked to say. *Just one spook at a time*. So long as we're doing that, and so long as I was a part of it, I'd be okay, too.

But something tugged at my newfound sense of satisfaction, probably the chronic sense of dissatisfaction with myself that rears its contrarian head at precisely the moments when I begin to feel smug.

This time, the tugging came from behind me. From the church.

I drifted through the brick walls and rose through the floor, emerging midway down the central aisle. The votive lights in their glass cups twinkled near the altar railing. A steady, fierce glow came from a reading light attached to the pulpit where Father Jenkins scratched at a piece of paper with a chewed-on pencil.

Behind him, a statue set in a small alcove by the altar had a bath towel curled around its head like a turban. None of his parishioners were going to confuse a broken shingle with a divine statement.

Spooks were scattered across the pews, many with the dazed expressions of newbies, a few with heads bent and hands clasped in prayer. Behind me, a couple of guys were taking turns diving into a hymnal lying on the bench. One popped from between the yellowed pages.

"I could swear I saw a road map in here, Artie. With rest-stops, scenic sights and spook-friendly places that had golden buckets."

"Keep looking, Mel. And don't swear. You'll jinx us if you swear in church."

Up front, the priest looked up from the pulpit. He swept the dark and (he thought) empty church with a steady gaze, raised his hands in a group-hug and said, "My friends, I know many of you are going through difficult times right now. So is this old church."

He looked down, shook his head. "Too defensive. Whimpering."

"Too vague," came a mutter from the darkened, spectral congregation. "Details, they'll want details."

As I glided to the front, Father Jenkins scribbled furiously on his paper, and when he next looked up, his face was stern.

"A GREAT man," he said, "a NOBLE man, one not of OUR FAITH, once said a HOUSE DIVIDED cannot stand. How much SADDER, how much more DOOMED FOR DESTRUCTION is the house with a HOLE IN ITS ROOF."

The priest shuddered. "Old Testament was never your strength, Jenkins," he told himself.

A spook of the female persuasion drifted up the aisle, respectfully raised her hand and when the prelate persisted in not seeing her, said, "Father, excuse me, but I was told the church had a nice guide book for us. Something with plenty of pictures, large letters and no hyperlinks. Would you know where they're stored?"

Father Jenkins hacked and jabbed with his pencil, revising his sermon yet again. I was shuddering as though I'd been suddenly pushed into cold storage.

Round words, Whiner had said. Round. Like the way the prelate had said *noble* and *doomed*.

Possibilities, hypotheticals and conjectures whirled through my thick brain. Mostly, though, I was embarrassed by my own idiocy. Specters Anonymous had taught me that so long as I thought I was the biggest, grandest, smartest spook this side of daisy roots, I was never going to achieve the true transcendence that would let me move on to whatever came after here.

Brother Randall had punched my buttons so expertly that I couldn't see beyond his effect upon my personal afterlife. Me, me, me, it was always about me.

With dull eyes, I stared at the pulpit as Father Jenkins looked up from his scribbling with a guilty look and said:

"My friends, we have two choices. We can increase our donations a little bit each week to fix the roof. Or we can start using umbrellas in church when it rains."

The ghostly congregation moaned. Several *poofed* off — probably to the Baptists — and a few simply zipped through the ceiling.

I rushed to the pulpit and whispered in the priest's ear: "Perfect. Go with that."

Father Jenkins rubbed a pale white hand across a clerical chin and smiled to himself.

I was back in the third floor of Margie's building faster than a sparrow can burp. Security lights in the storage rooms joined with the glow of the slumbering city through the windows to give a somber tone to the place. If this was going to be the site of mayhem, I wanted to have the right atmosphere.

For once, I was sorry I didn't have a bit of the Tosser in me. Rattling the metal shelves and scaring the begeezus out of Whiner and Sniveler would be better treatment than they deserved.

"Hey, in there," I shouted. "I want to talk to you."

"Oh, it's the Great God Ralph, come back with a revelation." It was amazing how fast Sniveler could go from a deep sleep to intense groveling. "Speak, my lord. We will cherish every word, even the prepositions. We will honor for all time each syllable, although some might sound like a cat with a hairball."

"I want you to talk to me."

"But we spoke to you before we went to our buckets. We always speak to you then."

"Well, I missed it. You'll have to start over."

"Our Ralph," Sniveler began.

Whiner jumped swiftly in: "who art forever online, hallowed be thy log-on —"

"Wait a minute. *Log-on?*"

"It's the new translation, Your Worshipfulness," Whiner said. "We want to stay relevant for the younger generation."

"You'll just love what we've done to the grace before meals," Sniveler said.

I think I overestimated their ability to focus on the afterlife's important lessons. And underestimated what the Great Divide would be like for the rest of us if I ever succeeded in freeing them from their ashtray-cage.

Residents of happily-ever-after are supposed to be beyond superstition, but I'll admit to crossing my fingers as I said: "This voice that spoke to you with the round words, did he ever pray with you?"

"With *us?*" Whiner was perplexed. "You mean when you weren't here, oh Divineness?"

"I mean at any time."

"He never prayed, *per se,*" Whiner said.

"Not *per se,*" Sniveler agreed.

"What do you mean?" I was getting a feeling that a bad moment was right around a corner.

"More like *begging forgiveness,*" Whiner said.

"What makes you say that?"

"He said, *I beg your forgiveness* a lot."

"I'll say. A lot."

The more I heard about the situation, the less sense it made. Why someone should apologize to Whiner and Sniveler when, based upon my earlier talks with them, they had gotten themselves into this mess.

"What did you say back to this voice?"

"I said it was no big deal," said the ever-ingratiating Sniveler.

"And I asked if there was something he could do about the poor ventilation," replied the always-aggrieved Whiner.

"And how did this voice answer?"

"He told us to shut up."

"Yeah, said he wasn't talking to us."

The mysterious visitor knew how to apologize and didn't like Whiner and Sniveler. I was beginning to want to meet this discerning entity.

"Spook or breather?" I asked. "Could you tell his plane of existence?"

"Well, if he could talk with one of us —"

"— then he had to be one of us," I finished.

The thread-like certainty that had started to wrap itself around me inside the church was beginning to fray. Herding cats was a breeze next to figuring out what's really going on in happily-ever-after, where you're not sure who you are, what you're doing here or where you're going. Then, add to that, the problems of trying to figure out the specters around you, and you begin to see the good sense of the sunshiners who hope the afterlife is just a matter of sticking your head in a hole in the ground and keeping it there until the end of time.

"Look, if I think of anything else, I'll get back to you."

"We'll be right here, Your Everlastingness," Sniveler said. "I'm on the final stanza of *A Mighty Firewall Is Our Ralph*."

"And this is going to be relevant to the new generation, too?"

"Yes, I'm changing the imagery from castles to password protection."

"Well, ah, good luck to you."

"If you're at any good parties," Whiner chimed in, "look for our friend with the round words."

Which, even for the peculiar, confined, two-dimensional world of spooks trapped inside an ashtray is an odd thing to say.

"What makes you think that person goes to parties?"

"Because every other word he said was about parties."

Sniveler jumped in in high aggrievement. "I'd hardly say *every other word*. That would have the fellow say things like: *Hello (party) how (party) are (party) you (party)*."

"Okay, every tenth word was *party*."

"Naw," Sniveler wasn't letting go. "Then you'd have conversations like: *Hello, how have you been lately. Wonderful weather we've been (party) having. How's your Aunt Katherine? Did she ever have that (party) wart at the end of her nose removed? I hope (party) it wasn't painful*."

Besides being allowed the occasional grand entrance, an advantage of being a divinity is that you're also allowed the quiet exit.

I exercised my option for an unobtrusive departure and floated through the door while Whiner and Sniveler were reviewing the practicality of a one-in-twenty invocation of *party*.

I might have drifted quickly through the other rooms on the floor with their metal shelves and their boxes of legal records, but a shadow on one of the boxes hissed at me.

Shade flew across the dimness and landed squarely inside my shirt pocket. *(Note to self: Where do these pockets keep coming from? How come Shade is the only one who ever notices them? And where do they go after Shade leaves? And how many specters can rumba on the head of a pin? How about on the point? Must find time to answer these eternal mysteries.)*

"How'd you get here?" I asked. "Who brought you?"

"I brought myself." Shade climbed to the edge of the pocket, the tip of his shadow at a jaunty angle. "It's about time I became a little more independent."

"Bravo for you."

I think Shade smiled back, but it's hard to read expressions on a shadow.

"Why'd you choose this place to come to?"

"Sitting in my nook by a canal, you hear things. And see things. You'd be amazed the people who think that just because they're alone, that means that nobody else is there."

"Fancy that."

"Once I even saw a man kill a woman."

"That's awful."

"Actually, it's worse." Shade pulled himself entirely out of my pocket and sat on the edge. "I saw them walking along the canal on many evenings. They would talk about getting married and raising kids. Then one night there was a big argument. She'd been offered a chance to exhibit her stuff in Philadelphia — she was an artist, you see — and she wanted to hold off on their engagement until after the exhibition. I think she was letting her beau down easily, that she wanted to cancel their plans entirely."

"And he killed her?"

"In front of my own astral eyes. There happened to be an empty boat nearby, and he put her body there, like she was dozing, and rowed away. That was the last I ever saw of him."

Too much time around Whiner and Sniveler, I'm afraid, had predisposed me to confusion. "I still don't see why that brings you here?"

"I've spent all these years wondering if that ghastly man ever received justice. Don't expect I'll ever learn that. But someone said that lady's work was here. I didn't really pay attention to it the first time you brought me here. I came back because I've never been around a famous artist before, leastwise, not one that I saw die. It's only respectful to pay attention to what she did."

"No, the least you can do is ignore it," I mumbled as I searched my memory. "I've been through all of the storage rooms on these floors. I haven't seen paintings or boxes large enough to hold any. Of course, if they were smaller they might be able to fit —"

"No, no," Shade said with a chuckle. "She was an artist, all right. But she didn't work with paint and canvas. She did her work with clay. She made ceramics."

$\mathcal{T}wenty\text{-}\mathcal{S}even$
CHAPTER

If feathers didn't pass through me, you might have knocked me down with one.

"This artist," I said. "Her name wouldn't be Letitia Sanderling?"

Shade bounded slightly on the lip of my shirt pocket. "Letitia. That's the name. What her last name was, I never knew. But Letitia. Who could forget a name like that?"

"You'll never believe what I've been doing," I said.

"Try me."

So I did. I told him about the two spooks trapped in a ceramic ashtray that was so *avant-garde* it was childish, about the mysterious rattling and thumping that came nearby when someone talked about parties, about the way that racket was ruining Margie's business and my transcendence. And, since I was disgorging myself already, I talked about the artist who could fashion cups and plates of such delicacy that they're now in museums, how she could also produce, at the peak of her career, absolute junk, and about why Letitia's lawyer could have kidded himself into believing that garbage would someday be so valuable that he was saving it.

"Remember I was in that ashtray during my last visit," Shade said. "Do you think you can catch a virus from pure ugliness? I haven't been feeling like myself since then."

When we passed through the door, Whiner and Sniveler, who'd been whining and sniveling at each other, went quiet.

"Me, again," I said. "And I've brought a friend."

More silence, this time with a sullen edge.

Be that way.

Shade flipped to my shoulder and surveyed the lumpish, off-center, unevenly-surfaced, wretchedly colored *objets d'art* crafted by one of the South's most skillful artists with a pottery wheel and a pile of clay.

"I don't remember that one over there," said Shade and pointed with a side of his shadow toward a purple-ish vase. Whatever it was, the vase had a lid leaning against its base.

"What about it?" I asked.

"Dunno. Could we check it out? Something tells me inside we're going to find…. I dunno. Something's there."

"Never hurts to look," I said with the jaunty confidence of a true idiot.

I dove toward the vase and felt Shade hop off my shoulder as my astral form tightened to fit through the opening. Even before I was completely inside, I could tell that Shade was on to something. The interior gave off a strange emanation. At first, I might have called it a scent or maybe a subtle vibration. But that wasn't it.

"You're right," I called up to Shade, who stood on the lip of the vase looking down at me. "Something's very wrong about this thing."

"Be careful," he said.

I compressed myself until the lip of the vase looked as though it were three or four stories above me. Shade flitted away, and I turned my attention to the interior.

The surface here was better than the outside, owing to some instrument used to smooth the clay. Still, I could see gouge marks and indentations from a tool.

During my time as a breather, I'd been in enclosed places where noxious odors made my head light and garbled my thoughts. This was something like that. But it also resembled times early in my specterhood when I ventured close to sunlight and felt the effects of a few gazillion photons on my ectoplasm.

"I'm coming out," I said. "Whatever's here is starting to get to me."

That's when the lights went out.

In a wink, the security lights inside the room were extinguished, and the glow of the window from street lamps, neon lights, office buildings and homes were muffled. Gone, kaput, nixed.

You'd think spooks wouldn't need night-lights, right? That it's silly to suggest specters wouldn't take to the dark like guppies to a pond? Get back to me about that when you find yourself in my neighborhood.

"Bad time for the power to go out," I mumbled.

I shot out through the top of the vase — at least, that was my plan, but my butt was soon whacking the bottom of that absurd, ugly container. Acting on instinct — which I'm much better at acting on than anything resembling a plan — I zipped out through the side of the container. Only, as zipping went, it was a failure. Back into the vase I ricocheted.

"Hah, hah, hah, hah."

Unless I was terribly confused, that wasn't my laugh. It curled my hair, then proceeded to curl my ears, my fingernails and my toes. That laugh wasn't from someone having a good time, but from someone looking forward to a great meal.

"Shade! Hey, Shade! Can you get me out of here? What's going on?"

"Hmmm?" A Voice replied, curious and bemused. (*Note to self: Find out how much you have to earn until your fun-times get upgraded from* amusement *to* bemusement.)

More cautiously than before, I floated to the top of the vase. When I reached the lid, my head banged against the ceramic cover.

"That went nicely," I told myself, wiping tears of pain from my eyes and pressing the ectoplasm back into my arm. "Exactly where I thought it would be."

"It's so gratifying to see a manly spook who's in control."

The Voice again, sounding a little wispy, a little superior. And all around me at once. I was surrounded.

"Well," I said, "I've learned that the afterlife is the wrong place to leave things to chance."

"And wise, too. My, my, you do have it all, don't you?"

I was still uncomfortable and disoriented, but now I had more reasons. I felt like I'd fallen into a bubble bath with a stranger.

As unobtrusively as I could while surrounded by a hidden Voice, I proceeded to pat my way around the vase's interior, a process that took only a couple minutes, although the vase's purring and moans were getting on my nerves.

I didn't completely lose hope of finding an exit until I was pressing my hands into the last remaining stretch of untouched interior at the very middle of the bottom.

"If that don't beat all," I said to myself.

"What's that, darling?"

I didn't trust this Voice: It was too feminine for a non-corporeal spirit. And I didn't like its purring.

"I seem to be trapped here," I said. "There's no way out."

"And your problem is —?"

"Have you ever heard of dermatological phosphorescence?"

"Anything like dermatological obsolescence? An old girl-friend of mine wore her skin for decades after it went out of style."

"It's related, but this is the phosphorescent variety."

"Phosphorous. That's like glowing. Which reminds me, darling. Would you ever so much mind patting me down again. I believe I've lost a comb in here somewhere."

Which begged the question of exactly where *here* was for my companion, who couldn't be hiding behind the smallest molecule in this place. Tangents, I was beginning to suspect, were the *modus operandi* for my vase-mate.

"Phosphorous can be like glowing," I began slowly, not having a clue where I was going. "It also can be like fireworks, like searchlights tearing through the sky, like high noon in the Sahara."

"Oh, dear. This is beginning to sound unpleasant."

"Specters afflicted with dermatological phosphorescence catch fire. They burn, they flare, they illuminate themselves with a fire that can be seen beyond the horizon. At least, that's what can happen under stress."

"Stress?"

"Yes." I felt quite cheery, not having to sweat ectoplasm because I could now see the end of the yarn. "I have this, this thing about enclosed spaces. Whenever I feel trapped, I break out into bonfires. Can't help myself."

A spook who'd once been either a carnival barker or a politician — I haven't yet figured out which — taught me the beauty of a well-aimed pause. So I lapsed into silence, counted to seven, and tried to keep the perkiness from my voice when I resumed:

"Was that flare mine? Oh, goodness, I hope not. I'm so sorry. Ever since the funeral, I've had this silly reaction to confinement. Like anyone has to worry about being buried twice. Such nonsense."

The purring traced the evolutionary continuum through hissing, catcalls, growls and, finally, a thunderous roar. I joined the spirit of the moment and shouted at the top of my voice for the police, the fire department, the paramedics, the SWAT team, the Marines, the eight-eyed globular enforcers from the Crab Nebula. And when I ran out of law enforcement figures, I screamed out the names of chess pieces. They've intimidated me since someone tried to teach me the game before I could write my own name.

I screamed my way through the primary colors and was working on the letters of the alphabet when Margie finally got the message that something was amiss and she wasn't going to get any sleep until she did something about it.

Abruptly, the vase's lid flew up and crashed with spectacular force, Margie's face popped into the opening, red-cheeked, red-eyed and red-foreheaded. I've said a couple hundred times that I was going to start my own searchlight repair shop before I'd willingly let another breather pass right through me, but when I shot out of that vase, I aimed at Margie's nose and didn't slow down until I hit the cumulus layer above Richmond.

Sometimes, you've just got to get everything out of your system. I drifted a while up there, with an ocean of darkness above and the muffled glow of the city below, and in the east, a subtle gleam began to mark the horizon. Dawn was probably less than an hour away.

Not much time to tie up a couple loose ends before getting back to Brother Randall's Camp for Wayward Spooks.

Margie was on her knees in the storage room, sweeping up the remains of the vase's lid that she'd thrown against a wall in her haste to get me and the Voice to shut up.

One little lid made a lot of debris. Then I realized what had happened. The lid hit the world's ugliest ashtray and both had exploded into bits of pottery, nuggets of colored clay and dust.

"Wait," I cried, "No," when I saw Margie head toward a garbage can with a dustpan of junk.

"Don't you start yelling again," she said.

"That's not trash," I said. "That's spooks."

"How can you tell?"

Margie was in no mood to be reminded that specters who invade the caskets, urns or mausoleums of other spooks have a tough time leaving. It wasn't until I'd been trapped inside the vase with the purring Voice that I managed to figure out what had happened to Whiner and Sniveler. And what made the vase, the ashtray and the other obnoxious pottery in the storeroom special.

I leaned over the vase. "Letitia? I know that's you in there, Letitia. You've got to talk to me."

"Will you come back inside if I do?"

"No."

Letitia managed to make her silence pout.

I added: "If you're not interested in bringing the man to justice who did this to you, that's your decision. I'll respect it. No nagging from me."

The vase rattled, a soft drum beat grew louder as the vase vibrated faster. I could have sworn I saw the sides of the vase tremble like an exhausted runner, and when Letitia found her voice, it was set at maximum volume.

"That snake. That maggot poop. That wart on the backside of creation. He's gonna answer for what he did to me."

"My thoughts exactly. But first you have to answer two questions."

Margie set down the dustpan and brush and edged closer to me and the vase. I motioned for her not to interrupt. She motioned that she didn't take orders from the likes of me.

"The man who did this to you," I asked Letitia. "It was your lawyer, wasn't it? R. Everette Johnston."

"That toad. That carbuncle. That lying, deceiving, murdering worm."

I tapped the vase to get Letitia's attention, then asked my second question: "What does the *R* stand for?"

Twenty-Eight

CHAPTER

etitia wasn't going to let a simple answer stand without amendment, elaboration, illustration and commentary. At least, I was saved from having to ask several dozen questions to understand what happened to Richmond's most famous ceramic artist and her lawyer-boyfriend.

They were only months from their wedding when they argued about a gallery's interest in showing Letitia's growing body of work. Letitia was overwhelmed by the prospect of acquiring a dealer and a husband at the same time and, being of a domestic inclination, decided to delay the showing until next season, whereas her beau believed they shouldn't turn down any offers that came with money attached.

One word led to another, as words often do. And two words led to a torrent, which words sometimes do. And the torrent led to violence, which torrents rarely do but when they do they get your attention.

My conversation with Shade allowed me to add the detail about the lawyer moving Letitia's body to a nearby boat. Letitia added the fact that her kiln was not far upriver. And the two of us reached the same conclusion — that the lawyer decided to destroy the evidence of the crime in the kiln, then mixed her ashes with clay to make amateurish figures and cookware.

"I'm sure he was concerned the police could analyze ash." Letitia sighed. "He was always a very thorough man."

"He still is." I surveyed the debris in Margie's dustpan from the shattered lid and the remnants of the world's ugliest ashtray.

"Would you mind a little company?" I asked Letitia.

"Gawd, if I spend one more minute wondering what my nails look like, I'll go mad. Bring 'em on."

The eastern sky was already beginning to take on subtle layers of gray when I rematerialized near Brother Randall's headquarters in the rail yard. Inside, the strange corridors that stretched forever — except when they looped in never-ending whorls — were eerily quiet. Time for all good spooks to hit their buckets, but I've learned from experience that not all spooks are good and even those most dedicated to moving away from their first lives can't resist the chance to watch sunrise sneak up on the horizon.

In the endless corridors of ceramic vases, everyone I peeked into was empty. A couple of spooks might be stupid enough to leave their buckets before sunrise. But a couple hundred? I wandered through the foggy corridors and soon discovered a sound, an indistinct noise that gradually revealed itself to be weeping.

Three quick turns brought me to the spook camp's decorously appointed office and Mrs. Pellywanger. Papers cascaded from her clipboard as, bent over, she comforted someone sobbing at her knees. I only saw a worn, disreputable coat, thread-bare shoes, a cowlick that seemed to be on the wrong head, but, for me, that was enough.

"Fast Eddie, what are you doing here? What's wrong?"

I wish I had a camera when Fast Eddie turned around. Heck, I wish my mother and all the friends who said I'd never amount to anything were there. The look on his face started at surprised and in half a heartbeat zoomed past ecstatic.

"You're okay," Fast Eddie said. "You're okay."

"Find a way for me to win the lottery and I'll be great," I said. "Meanwhile, I'll be okay."

"I didn't mean to do it to you, Ralphie. I swear, I didn't know what was going on."

One more *Ralphie* and I was going to start taking hostages, but for the moment, I decided to be gracious. "You've never hurt me, pal."

"But using my old Tosser powers. Moving that lid onto that vase. They told me it was a joke. I didn't know the vase was part-spook."

Fast Eddie turned his weepy, pitiful face toward Mrs. Pelly, who stroked his knobby gray head as though he were a kitten.

"All's well, dearie, just like I told you," she whispered to Fast Eddie. "And now your friends are here just in time to see the sacrifice."

"Sacrifice?" That word sounded familiar, but I couldn't place it.

"A friend of his was selected by Brother Randall for a great honor." Mrs. Pelly looked up. "That's the other reason the poor thing is crying. He's weeping for joy."

Fast Eddie's face, when he turned toward me, was ravaged, barely recognizable. "I tried to stop him, Ralph. Not at first, maybe. But I did try later."

"To have someone close to you be involved in such a noble purpose," Mrs. Pelly said. "He is making a leap for the angels.'

"*Noble purpose. Leap for the angels.* Will someone talk English?"

Mrs. Pelly patted Fast Eddie's head. "A sacrifice. One of your friends is making a sacrifice at sunrise."

I had the image of Hank placing a fatted calf on a makeshift altar, but that didn't make any sense. I looked at Fast Eddie. His eyes were glowing so brightly now that I saw little clouds of ectoplasm steaming away from his cheeks and nose.

"I thought they were giving Cal a medal or something," he said. "I didn't know they were going to ——"

Mrs. Pelly touched Fast Eddie with the gentleness of a grandmother. "That's what sacrifices are for, little one."

I was out of there quicker than half a sputter from a burning fuse. I zipped through the train station, eyes straining at the platforms that were filling up with passengers watching the tracks. When I looped through Shockoe Slip and came back from the east, I noticed the specters in brown monk's robes assembled on the concrete yard outside.

They stood in the shadows cast by the tired-brick clock tower while, in the distance on the other side of the building, the sun marshaled its forces for its daily assault on the world. A vast spectral multitude stood in the yard or floated atop each other, with dozens sunk into the ground so only their heads emerged to watch the show.

I swooped down to a knot of my friends.

Gilda was glaring at Hank and Gwendolyn. "What's this about Cal?" I asked Gilda. "He's making some sort of sacrifice?"

"Cal *is* the sacrifice," Gilda shot back.

"What?" I heard, but I didn't hear.

Hank rubbed a hand across his face. "Remember Randall sounding off last night? About purifying the faithful for letting those Confederates chase him off Libby Hill? That's what it's about."

"But we're dead," I shouted. "What are they going to do? Shoot us?"

Gwendolyn jabbed his cigar over his shoulder. Emerging from blackened tiles on the western-facing roof of the tower, his arms crossed over his chest with a nonchalance I've never seen before, was Cal. His eyes drifted over the crowd before they settled on me and my friends.

Slightly below the roof, but still shielded by the tower from the growing effects of the dawn was a phalanx of Randall's bulkier followers.

"He'll be okay for a couple minutes after sunup," Hank said. "But soon, the sun will rise a little higher, the shadows on the western side of the building will dissolve, and Cal will be exposed to full sunlight."

"But he can leave. He can *poof* away at any time. Now, or seconds before the sun gets too strong."

Hank widened his stance. "That only works if Cal wants to leave."

"Then we don't give him a choice. We go up there and haul him down. There's enough of us. We can do it."

"Take another look," Gwendolyn said.

I noticed the base of the tower. Several dozen of Randall's goonies were loitering in the deepest shadows.

"We've got to do something," I said. "We're running out of time."

"Randall's thugs are going to sit on the chest of any spook who interferes," Hank said. "Sit there until the sun rises and the light boils away anyone who's interfering into paranormal NeverNeverLand. The goons will get their reward in their next afterlives."

"No," I shouted. "I won't let them."

"Uber-Spirit," Gilda said, "help me to do the things I can do —"

Hank joined in, "— to stop trying to do the things I cannot do —"

And, for the big finish, all chimed, "— and to give me a slap upside the head to quit analyzing the previous requests."

This was one of those third cases, the ones that need a whack between the eyes, although, when Randall drifted through the bricks of the clock tower, it wasn't my own head I was thinking about whacking.

"I think I'm going to have a little chat with the boss," I said, nodding toward Randall.

"Very sensible," Hank said. He moved closer. "But the Ralph I know isn't acquainted with *sensible*. He doesn't do *sensible*. He wouldn't know *sensible* if he fell into a barrel full of *sensible*."

"Oh, ye of little self-actualizing affirmation," I said.

Slowly, so as not to perturb the great leader or his spookguards, I drifted from the edge of the crowd toward the clock tower's roof where Randall hovered ten or fifteen feet below Cal.

"Oh Great Wonderfulness," I shouted as I approached the spookhead. "It is I, your faithful spy, come to give a final report."

A furrow cut across Randall's godly brow. His eyes darted over hundreds of robed followers watching from the ground by the railroad station. "Er, don't you think this conversation should be a little more private?"

"Yes, but I won't let that get in my way. We spies, you see, can be very determined."

"Shhh," he shhhed. "Don't use that word."

I could have sidled closer. In fact, I'm sure Randall would have been willing to make room for me inside his glorious robe. Instead I hovered thirty or forty feet away.

"What I have to say," I said, "should be known to all your slack-brained subjects."

"My what?"

"I have found a threat to your plans, your dreams, your everlasting existence."

I'll give Randall credit. He must have had several quarts of embalming fluid in his system to stay so cool. "An army approaches?" he asked. "Perhaps several armies?"

"No, a single creature."

"Not the bird again," he snarled.

"No." I didn't bother to fight my smile. "A woman."

A faint glow rose in his eyes. "A woman. What woman? Where?"

"At this hour, your mightiness, I suspect she's already in her bucket."

Randall looked perplexed. A couple of spooks in the support beams of the overpass giggled. I detected a rustling spread through the faithful below. No doubt, they felt I was long overdue for being smited back into my place.

"If someone won't get out of her bucket," the great one intoned, "I don't see how she could be party to any substantial threat."

"Funny choice of words there, Your Loftiness. *Party* and *substantial*. They sound so... round."

"What does that have to do with this spectral sister who will not leave her bucket?"

"She's not leaving her bucket, oh Splendiferous One, because she seems to be the bucket. Or, more properly, the vase. Her non-corporeal essence was mixed with the clay and the water that formed that vase."

"The plans of the Uber-Spirit are truly inscrutable," he said, growing uneasy. "In the fullness of time, we may come to understand. If not, we must still accord that vase — wherever it is, assuming it exists at all — with the full respect due any of our numbers. That vase has run its race and fought the good fight."

"But why are we asking this poor specter"— I pointed grandly to Cal, who hovered above me near the top of the tower, where the tiles are taking on the pink tinge of dawn —"this poor, miserable, despicable spook, to make himself a sacrifice? Should we not bring that other poor specter, forever entombed in a ceramic prison, here instead? She's a more worthy opponent. Wouldn't that make her a better sacrifice?"

"How can we sacrifice a vase? It is of the material world." Randall gathered his voice for the benefit of the crowd, but I was close enough to read the worry in his squinty little eyes. "Will it not cast a shadow? Can it not be seen in a mirror? If a breather kicks it, will not his toe be sorely afflicted? And if we consort with it, will we not slide ever closer to perdition and sunshine?"

"But it's more than a vase. There's a specter inside. She remembers, she is aware of events on the astral plane, she feels and speaks." That one struck home with the noble kahuna, so I repeated: "Boy, does she ever speak."

Randall's hands were shaking now. He blinked, sunup was close; tics rippled across his face. I needed more time to hack away at this tottering ego. Blunt force, even of the verbal variety, carries its risks, but I was running out of time for my own version of subtlety.

"Bet you could use a good lawyer," I observed. "One who can smother you in so many words no one can ever recognize you."

"I was a good lawyer." Randall's lips trembled and a twitchy muscle in his cheek twisted a corner of his mouth into a sickly smile.

"But you weren't a very good potter."

Five or six stories above the concrete yard of the railroad station, we glared at each other, Randall and I. Below us a deathly silence spread over the assembled spooks, and when folks who've been the centerpiece of a funeral have a deathly silence, even the breeze decides to go elsewhere without any fuss.

I heard the gigantic metal lungs of an approaching railroad engine wheeze like a long-distance runner; its wheels clattered and rumbled on the rails leading to the platforms below.

"I didn't want it to turn out like this," Randall whispered. "But he made me. He made me attack my dearly beloved Letitia. He told me to put her body in the kiln. And, once I entered the afterlife myself, he told me that the time for penance had arrived. I would have to atone for my sins by leading the army he had spent ages gathering. Lead them until all opposition within the afterlife is eliminated and he — and he, alone — would be the master here."

I was confused, and Cal was running out of time. "Who do you mean?"

"Him!" Randall's eyes were wide, his body moved like a corpse. "The deceiver. The great betrayer. The father of lies."

There was a slight rustle at the edge of Randall's shirt collar. Peering up at me, Shade said, "Did someone mention my name?"

Shade was cool, he was cocky, he was smug and in control. If I thought it wouldn't distract Randall, I'd try to throttle the afterlife out of that vicious speck of darkness.

Fortunately for Shade, Randall roared at his goons on the ground to get Cal to safety. Cal stuck to his guns. Or, his roof. Two of Randall's muscle-spooks had to drag Cal back down.

Shade hopped onto my shoulder as a deep blush spread across the eastern sky and the crowd of spooks jammed beneath the underpass grew fidgety. Full sunlight was minutes away. But, if the crowd left too soon, they'd miss more drama than had come to happily-ever-after since the night an old-timer named Frederick managed to find a way to ignite his own beard with St. Elmo's fire.

"You're good," Shade said. "You didn't bat an eye when I told you Letitia's sad, sad story. But you were putting together the pieces all along."

"I'm a spook. I like flying under the radar."

"Have you ever thought about management?" Shade whispered to me. "I'm talking about the top of the executive ladder. Starting at the last rung and working your way even higher."

"That's exactly what I intend to do," I said.

"Oh, I can predict a wonderful, dark future for you." Shade was all smiles, except for the part that was nearly curtsying with excitement. "I have gathered an army that lies just outside the city. With you at its head, there is nothing in this world or any other world to stop us."

"I hate to be blowing my own horn," I replied, "but that sounds like the absolute truth."

Contempt radiated from Shade's tiny dark figure as Randall cupped his head in his hands, softly muttering, "Letitia, Letitia, what have I done?" drifted to the ground and, without pause, sank into it. In seconds, even the black enameled hair was a frightful memory.

"Come on," Shade told me. "If we hurry, we can find a bucket with our troops in the countryside. At first darkness today, we'll be on the march. And, before the sun rises again, we'll be masters of this city."

"There I have a little problem with your plan. *Transcendence*, as a friend of mine likes to say, *involves staying in your own socks*."

"What the Roth does that mean?"

"I don't have the slightest idea. But if I stay around these good spooks"— I gestured toward the horde watching quietly from the rapidly shrinking shadows in the rail yard —"I think I might actually find out some night."

Twenty-Nine
CHAPTER

he last I saw of Shade, he was winging like a heavily caffeinated butterfly toward the James River where, from the deep shadows underneath the trees on the opposite shore, members of his ghostly legion beckoned for him to hurry.

Our paths are bound to cross some night on the astral plane. Shades, I've come to learn, are hard to get rid of.

When the first photons bounced off the clock tower, those of us gathered outside the Richmond train station raced toward the nearest structure that offered protection from the approaching day — Brother Randall's Religious Retreat and Crash Pad.

A blizzard of papers flew from Mrs. Pellywanger's clipboard as she directed the in-coming horde to empty containers for the day. Mrs. Pelly may have stepped in over her head, employment-wise, four or five jobs ago, but she was at her best in a crisis.

With the efficiency of an old-time letter sorter, she sent everyone from the St. Sears group to the far right corner of one corridor, my favorite gaggle of touring Cincinnati spooks down another, with other directions for spirits based upon their Specters Anonymous affiliation, tolerance to noise, self-control around strangers, and preferences for buckets (ceramic, glass, metal, Tupperware or other).

Studying me, she stabbed the edge of her clipboard toward a corridor that, judging by its unpopularity, must be reserved for spooks who carried their old skin conditions into the hereafter.

"You," she said, "go there."

I looked around for moral support, but my friends from the St. Sears group were trudging the path to happy naptime in other directions, and I was left to face alone the sentence imposed upon prophet-slayers.

The corridor led me to a set of glass doors that opened with an automatic hiss that was probably as welcoming as a hiss could get. A half-dozen spooks working behind sleek blonde-wood desks looked up when I entered. A few rose, some continued working and one specter prostrated himself on the floor. He must have been a newbie, because he soon shot straight through the ceiling.

Well, I never liked boot-lickers anyway.

"Carry on," I told them. "You're helping the transcendence of our brethren. And sistern."

Some of the workers clasped their hands as tears streamed down their cheeks, while others rolled their eyes and kept working. The fellow who'd drifted into the ceiling, whom I saw as the tie-breaker, gave a moan loaded with ambiguity.

Any illusions of grandeur lasted not quite as long as a single flicker from a candle.

"Do we genuflect, Your Ralphness, or would you like me to kiss your backside," said Gilda.

She stood in the doorway with a blank look that even the automatic dooropener understood meant that obsolescence was the price for getting in her way.

"Calling me *Ralph* would do nicely."

"Your every commandment is my wish."

"Actually, you've got that backwards."

"No, I've got that sideways."

Gilda fixed me with a look that, in another time, would have encouraged me to change planes of existence. Too late I realized that if I hadn't faced down Brother Randall, he'd be the one who had to deal with this Goth-sized attitude disguised as a specter.

"You don't think I really meant what I said out there, do you?" I stammered. "You can't be serious. Would I believe Shade's offer of commanding an army to take over the afterlife? Who'd follow me into battle? Heck, nobody would follow me across the street to smell a fresh batch of chocolate chip cookies at the diner."

A verbal death dart rose from Gilda's spleen (*Note to self: Next opportunity, go to the medical college and research this spleen thing. Why should an anatomical organ only grow in the abdomens of characters in certain genres of fiction?*), and I watched with genuine fascination as she cogitated over her answer.

I'd like to think my behavior during the last hour earned some respect in her eyes, or perhaps I was just too easy a target at the moment, but the wrinkle of a grin appeared in the corner of her mouth.

Gilda asked, "Are we talking chocolate chip cookies with macadamia nuts?"

"Is there any other kind?"

Gilda and I drifted into the corridor together. Behind us in Randall's office, the clicking and clacking and muttering and murmuring of an urban work place resumed, along with one puzzled voice whimpering. I was sure it was the newbie who'd melted into the ceiling: whether he was kicking himself for acting like a jerk in the presence of a deity or was suddenly overcome by the realization that idiots can come within a whisker of seizing world power, I can't say.

"Let me show you where the peons' buckets are," Gilda said.

I shouldn't admit it, but there was something appealing now about Brother Randall's old headquarters, an aura rooted in the dusky light and the fog crawling through the corridors that might be chiseled from stone or, perhaps, merely random openings that appear in the mist.

A pleasant feeling welled up from those shadows, something akin to walking along the canal on a moonless night. Magical. Even specters enjoy quiet moments that carry the promise of things beyond the limits of the merely paranormal.

I knew that I'd never felt so secure during daylight hours because the darkest house has cracks and crevices and ill-fitting blinds. Not Brother Randall's old haunt. (*Sorry about that.*) I felt like a kid whose parents allowed him to stay up until midnight.

A child, the mysterious realm that opens to the world when the clock strikes twelve, the accepting smile of a parent — the tableaux started to coalesce in the darkness. And I knew I was on the verge of another revelation about my own past.

A revelation that involved a car, whose hard rubber steering wheel I could nearly feel beneath my finger tips.

"Hey, guys." Hank beckoned from the end of a corridor. "In here."

When we reached him, Hank stepped into the wall, and Gilda and I followed.

That put us in a vast cavern with a strangely angled floor, where every spook I'd seen outside had gathered. In the back, against the wall, a detachment of rebel soldiers practiced their parade-ground maneuvers.

"Hi, I'm Cal. And I'm a gratefully confused specter."

With those words, every spook in the hall turned to my sponsor. Cal floated slightly above the floor at the far end of the room: He was whole again, unconflicted, his arms were crossed over his chest, his eyes studied the design of the floor. The quiet humility of his presence screamed: *Here is a specter who'll only open his mouth when there's something important to say, something meaningful to tell his fellow spooks.*

"I have many things in my afterlife that make me say, *Thanks a bunch.*" Cal spoke in a soft voice that filled the chamber. "But until a few minutes ago, I never realized I should be grateful for confusion. Before, I thought that if I didn't have the answer to every question, I should be embarrassed. It was something to hide.

"Yes, I know others aren't confused because they have the answers to all the great questions. I'm happy for my friends who have that certainty. Powerfully, genuinely, down-to-my-socks happy for them, without the tiniest bit of smugness or superiority. That's because I'm a little envious.

"But I'm not going to be sorry that I'm confused. I'm going to be grateful for that, too. Because that shows I'm still open to the leadings of the Uber-Spirit, or universal life force, or the next wild-eyed spook who shows up at a Specter's Anonymous meeting and thinks he's got all the answers."

Cal looked up, his eyes clear, his glance steady. "Who'd like to share what our literature calls their *perplexities, tremors and fantasies?*"

Gilda and I hung around as the meeting unwound in that cavern. I felt a strong sense of security among spooks who were helping each other sort through the chaos of the astral plane, and secretly pleased to see a gleam in Gilda's eye, a quickness in her movements. Perhaps even Goths could come to believe that the afterlife had some relevance to them.

"And to think," I said, "if I'd only helped Father Jenkins a couple nights ago with his building fund, none of this would have happened."

"Yeah, that's something," Gilda said. She smiled to herself while we turned into another foggy hallway. Somehow, she left that lazy smile behind at the corner.

"I don't understand." Gilda turned on me. "How would helping the priest have changed anything?"

"I wouldn't have been around for this crisis." I spread my hands and gave her my best what-a-wacky-afterlife shrug, but Gilda didn't seem to be into chivalry at the moment. And why should she?

As we wandered the misty corridors to the jars where we could spend the day, I thought about the dark pall cast over her nights for the last week, being up close and way too personal with Brother Randall, watching Cal slowly erode into a handful of ectoplasm, and I recognized my role in the misunderstandings we'd had lately. She was a spook of the formerly estrogen-carrying variety, and I couldn't treat her like Hank or Gwendolyn. I had to be more feeling-oriented, more concerned about her emotional life, more supportive.

So I told her how pleased I was with the animation and — dare I say it? — *the life* that I saw in her now. And that I was going to be more attentive to her feelings and her thoughts and our relationship and the other mush that's important to formerly female spooks.

Gilda turned on me a look that was all Goth. "Puh-LEEES," she said and darted into her bucket.

I spent a perfectly restful day in my jar, and when I awoke with the certainty that a cool blanket of darkness had settled over the city, Mrs. Pelly was waiting for me in the corridor, a fully loaded clipboard clenched in her hand.

"Before you go," she said, "I was wondering if you'd take a moment to fill out our customer satisfaction survey."

She handed me a piece of paper, which drifted through my fingers to the floor. 'Natch. She was a typical *two-fer*, always forgetting which plane of existence she was dealing with.

She put on a brave smile. "I hope we can count on your future business and your recommendation to your friends."

"You're at the absolute top of my list."

The run-in with Mrs. Pelly reminded me of a loose end with another *two-fer*. I knew that if I could locate the cavern where Cal held the meeting last night, I'd find spooks still there, but I set my sights on Margie's.

Richmond's newest psychic was in the front room of her little suite that served as the waiting room for her clients. In one hand was the world's ugliest flower vase, in the other, a handful of dead flowers.

"I really wish you'd knock," she said.

"Okay." I floated through the door and said, "Knock, knock."

"Who's there?"

"Your favorite spook."

"Come on in, Hank."

Not quite the greeting I was looking for, but it got me inside. I studied the vase as she set it on the window sill, then began putting the dead flowers into the vase with the care of a professional florist. Permit me to be clear, when I said the flowers were dead, I meant the petals were wilted and the leaves crackled and fell apart if Margie brushed against them.

"Where'd you get those?" I asked.

"From the flower shop down the street," she answered spritely. "They were on sale."

"Did you save that broken ashtray?" I asked.

"Every last flake."

An unfortunate word — *flake* — but maybe the best word. "What'd you do with it?"

"I put it in there." Margie nodded to the vase, Letitia's vase, the same vase into which she was placing the black stems of dead flowers.

"It's really quite yummy, darling." Letitia's voice rose from the narrow mouth of the container. "Having a man or two around the old place again."

"No, ma'am, the pleasure is all ours." That would be Sniveler.

"Could we have a tad less water in here?" And Whiner.

As I looked at the misshapen vase and heard the jumble of voices rising from the interior, I also saw the dead flowers fill out before my eyes, brimming with the power of the afterlife.

The night stretched before me, but I was aching with a desire to be with Petey that felt almost physical. One advantage of having a beagle as your friend is that they're not grumpy if you wake them in the middle of the night to talk. Eternal optimists, they're always confident that any break in routine will involve a snack.

As I sped over Libby Hill and saw the lights gleaming from the porch of Petey's duplex, I also noticed a commotion around the base of the obelisk at the Confederate memorial. I wheeled down for a look.

The colonel greeted me with a solemn dip of his chin. "The enemy looks to be decamping," he said.

I followed his gaze to the trees and homes on the eastern horizon. I couldn't see anything out of the ordinary, but then, I wasn't a professional military man.

"When do you get to go home?" I asked.

He answered with the slightest smile. "I'm there now."

I left the old soldier to his quiet patrol and drifted over to a group of spooks who were jabbering and gesturing at once. A palpable excitement rose from the crowd. Heads turned toward me, hands waved. I recognized some of the faces from the Poe museum and Brother Randall's compound.

"There he is," was the common refrain. Followed by, "Mr. Poe. Mr. Poe." And more broad smiles and waves.

A single figure slipped from the crowd, and a young spook of the female inclination came toward me. Her eyes were a shade of blue that banished the night.

She stopped a few feet from me and my heart — wherever it was — did a couple flips.

"So nice of you to come say good-bye, Mr. Poe," Miss Blue Eyes said. "It means so much to me and my friends."

"I couldn't allow my favorite people from Cincinnati to leave without a word or two." If I had real shoes, I'd be scuffing them in the grass by now. "Where are you going?"

"Paris," she said, brightly. "None of us has ever been to Paris. And, since no one has any pressing engagements at the moment, we thought this would be a good time to go. Why don't you come with us, Mr. Poe?"

"I can't leave here right now." I caught myself before I added, *Aw shucks*, and instead admitted, "I don't know how to tell you this, but I'm not really Edgar Allan Poe."

"We know." The smile grew brighter. "We're not really from Cincinnati."

Someone shouted, "Wagons, ho," and in groups of six or eight, the spooks rose from the hill.

Picture, if you will, a line of Conestoga wagons rising up from a hill, one-by-one, and circling slowly in the dark sky, then take away the wagons and the horses. What's left is what I saw above me as the little blue-eyed spook rose to join the last spectral wagon.

I floated toward the edge of the hill and shouted: "Where are you really from?"

"Akron. We just like to pretend we're from Cincinnati."

I drifted off the hill. The James River sparkled with chilled moonbeams. To the west, the city glowed like banked embers.

Again I shouted, "What's your name?"

"It's Nelle."

"Of course," I muttered, "I should have known."

Soon, a single voice rose in song from the specters heading toward the dark reaches of the east, then another, and soon the entire group was singing, although I couldn't make out their words until they reached the chorus:

"Why, oh. Why, oh. Why, oh. Did I ever leave Ohio?"

And I floated there on the sleepy border of the city until the last voice faded behind the black curtain of the horizon, and, like a stream of fireflies curlicuing through the night, those hardy pioneers slipped from view.

— The End —

Phil Budahn

**

A preview follows of
The third book in the Specters Anonymous series

The Infernal Task of Amon T. Lado

Available on Kindle and at Amazon.Com
Beginning Oct. 31, 2014

Currently available is the first book in the series, *Specters Anonymous.*

Check out our website at SpectersAnonymous.Com

**

The Infernal Task of Amon T. Lado
By Phil Budahn
Chapter One

The mist coming off the James River was so thick you could cut it with a knife. You'd probably want to use a ladle, though, and shove it around so you could see the hand in front of your face. Even then, you couldn't be sure it was your own hand.

I had pulled the early shift along Boulevard Bridge. Most high-pocket Richmonders had already gone home to Westover Hills. No one else was around to hear a rattle-trap of a pickup come roaring from the north shore. You know the kind, a five-thousand-dollar sound system on a machine worth less than the bobble-head doll glued to the dashboard.

House of the Rising Sun blared from the open windows at a volume that cleared the roadway of fog. I drifted through the guardrails and didn't feel safe until the slick gray waters of the James River rushed thirty feet below my feet.

Where the girl came from, I can't say. One minute, bare concrete roadway was in the middle of the bridge, licked by the occasional tongue of mist. The next moment, the single working headlight on the pickup flashed across this girl. She was kneeling in the middle of the concrete. Her head down, her face hidden by long brunette hair, her fingers spread on the ground as though she'd never seen asphalt before.

She didn't look up until the last second.

I'll hand it to the kid. As someone who's seen my share of banged-up bumpers hurtling toward my own head, I can tell you it takes a couple gallons of ice water in your trousers to stand your ground in that situation.

I've seen my quota of road kill, too, so I won't take any guff for choosing to study the streetlamps on the south end of the bridge until the rust-bucket thundered past. The pickup's woofers were set at maximum woof, and I think the echo of one line — *It's been the ruin of many a poor boy* — must have taken a day and a half to work its way out of the river system.

Let's not forget the poor girls, I thought.

Sentiment never paid the undertaker, still the poor kid in the road was entitled to have the only soul in the area wish her *bon voyage*. You owe them that much, right?

I drifted back through the guardrail and floated across the highway, not in any hurry to itemize the damage. Besides, a memory was tugging at me somewhere between the ears. Playing peek-a-boo. The recollection of a traffic accident where I might have received my expiration stamp.

Imagine my surprise when I reached the scene of the accident and the girl was still kneeling there. Except now her head was up, her eyes were as wide as a startled puppy's and I could see her stomach and shoulders shaking as wave after chilly wave swept over her.

"Just relax," I told her. "It'll be gone in a few seconds."

"I've never been this cold before." Her lower lip trembled a couple times. "I think that truck ran right over me. No, that's not right. It ran *through* me."

I looked at those big eyes, then at the nice lips. This wasn't the moment for explanations about what happens at the confluence of a non-corporeal entity with a physical source of energy or sentience. Besides, I'd lose what little respect I'd managed to achieve from my buddy Hank if word ever got out about me talking like that.

"Don't sweat it," I said. "Can you get up?"

"I... I think so."

She didn't do a bad job at it — getting up, I'm saying. She didn't do a good job of it, either. When she straightened, her feet decided it would be fun to go splashing in the water. And she sank through the bridge, feet-first.

I'll give her this: she sank like a lady.

"Just tell yourself it's time to get back on the bridge," I said.

"What's happening to me?" The frayed edges of panic crept into the corners of her eye. "This isn't supposed to happen, is it?"

"Takes a little getting used to. Don't try to figure it out. Just let yourself know you want to stand on top of the concrete now."

Soon she was back where she started, but this time she overshot actual contact with the bridge by about six inches. Still, not bad for a newbie. She was sporting a hesitant grin.

"Is this where I click my heels together three times and say, *There's no place like home?*"

"How about mumbling, *There's no place like the surface of the bridge?*"

"Okay, I'll try that."

She didn't have much to say as we crossed the bridge to the north shore and, eventually, wound our way through the towering tree trunks of Maymont Park. *Companionable*, I think, would be the word to describe that moment. It was comfortable being with her, although I knew her mind had to be racing like a hamster who'd been sipping from the coffee pot.

I was doing the hamster trick, too. Keeping the ol' mental gears spinning so they didn't have time to think about my own memory of a car wreck.

"I feel that I ought to be asking you a hundred questions," she said.

"Go ahead."

"You won't think I'm crazy, will you, just because my questions are a little crazy?"

"It's entirely possible I may run into the night, howling like a banshee." I said it with an ain't-I-silly tone. But it wasn't a joke, not entirely.

She was pretty good at reading nuances. She didn't say another anything else until we reached the manicured lawn of Byrd Park where Boulevard became a serious urban artery again.

By then, a prickly feeling was racing up and down the back of my neck. We let a few cars pass, I did this slow spin, trying to convince myself that we weren't being followed, and she experimented with a bush by the road. Inching a finger to a leaf, she tried to push it gently, so her finger didn't end up popping right through the plant.

Without looking at me, off-handedly, as if she was really more interested in finding a way to prod the leaf, she said, "I'm dead, aren't I?"

"It's like I said. Don't try to figure out anything right now."

"But I am dead." Not a question this time. And her eyes flashed and hit mine with a slap that could have awakened the living.

"Let's just say you've found the perfect way to hold down your spending."

She didn't object, didn't react at all, when I took her hand and we rose fifty or sixty feet into the sky. The fog lay below like a gigantic bag of cotton balls: toward downtown, the smaller buildings were glowing patches in the haze, while the upper floors of the tallest structures stretched into the clear night.

I thought open air would be the perfect cure for that itchy feeling on the back of my neck, the kind I usually get when a stadium-full of observers are watching me, but it only got worse.

"Where are we going?" she asked.

"I'm meeting some friends. Maybe you'd like to join us."

"*Meeting with friends.* I like that. So down-to-earth."

"As it were."

"Yes."

She had a nice smile. The wind didn't ruffle the smallest hair on her well-groomed head: she looked nice, what with the quarter moon gleaming in the background and the glow from downtown Richmond reflecting from her cheeks.

"I guess you already know who I am," she said.

"Actually, I don't know a thing about you."

"My name is Sheila. That's Sheila —" If I didn't know the confusion that was going through the kid at that moment, I would have described her expression as cute. But I did know. And, for once, I managed not to think of a smart-aleck remark.

"I'm from —" she started again, then looked up at me as though I should know. "I don't seem to remember my last name. Or where I'm from. Is this supposed to happen? It doesn't feel right."

"Just take it one night at a time," I said, echoing one of the program's mantras. "If you can manage that, you'll be okay."

Slowly, sadly, Sheila shook her head. "I don't think I can do that."

"Do you think you can go sixty seconds without breaking out into the wailing heebie-jeebies?" I asked.

"I can manage sixty seconds." She was watching me closely. "What happens after that?"

"Then we see if you can manage another sixty seconds."

Sheila's grip on my hand loosened. She seemed to relax and enjoy the ride. nd I felt like a dope for ever thinking the program's slogans were silly.

Well, maybe not for the saying that says, *blink, blink, blink*. I'm still trying to gure out what that's about.

After coasting over downtown, I put us on a glide path along Broad Street and Church Hill. Touchdown was next to steps that led to the basement room of a chapel set on a leafy side street.

My buddy Hank gave me the thumbs-up at the door. "Atta-boy, Ralph. You got a newbie. That's going to get you out of the cellar with Cal."

Hank had a chocolate complexion and a pigtail on the back of his head that gave our formerly feminine members hot flashes.

"Well," I said, "Cal ought to worry about getting out of my cellar."

Hank shot me a look. It wished me good luck with whatever's left after Cal cut me down to size.

Sliding through the door, I saw Cal at his usual gray metal chair. His arms were crossed over his chest, his head was bent down, and he gave me one of those I'm-not-looking-at-you looks.

I nudged Sheila toward him. Without quite looking at him, either, I said, "Cal, this is Sheila. She just arrived in town. I'm bringing her to her first meeting."

"Nice to meet you, Sheila," he says, cool as an eskimo's urn. "Let me introduce you to Gilda."

Gilda was our resident Goth. The rare problems that Hank couldn't settle get referred to Gilda. Any spook partial to black leather with chains, purple fingernails, industrial-black eye-liner and pasty white makeup tends to get her way.

"Pleased," Gilda said.

"Maybe you two can talk after the meeting," Cal said to Gilda. "Show Sheila the layout here."

"That would be so sweet," Sheila gushed.

Gilda answered with a smile-wince, which, on second thought, could have been a wince-smile. Gilda was no more likely to take suggestions and mingle with her fellow specters than any other member of the posthumous fellowship who thought bicycle chains were a fashion accessory.

But even a Goth can come to recognize that she has more problems with her own thought processes than mere blood loss. None of us were going anywhere so long as we took our own splendid advice about how to run an afterlife.

Sheila was now, to coin a phrase, Gilda's problem. I settled above the chair between Cal and Fast Eddie as Sheila took the chair between Cal and Gilda. Things were looking good. The funny feeling about being followed was gone. had shown Cal that I was helping the poor, still-suffering spook, while managing to avoid any chance of having a newbie drifting around, under, over and occasionally through me.

Sheila's immediate problem involved verticality. By the time Rosetta called the meeting to order, Sheila was coming to learn not to sink too far into the chair nor rise too often through the ceiling.

"My name is Rosetta," our erstwhile chairspook said. "I'm a recovering specter. Is anyone within their first thirty years of transcendence? Or, perhaps, attending their first meeting of Specters Anonymous?"

Sheila raised a tentative hand. "My name is Sheila. And I just arrived."

There was a smattering of "Welcome."

A few "Hi's."

A majority of "Keep coming back."

And Hank's inimitable, "Yo, there."

Sheila relaxed. "I'd like to say that I had no idea it would be so much like home to be in"— She looked at me, she gazed across the room, tears welled in her eyes —"in heaven."

- End of Sample -

Acknowledgements

The author gratefully acknowledges the support, critiques and occasional tough-love of his writer's group buddies, Rebecca Ruark, Carol Rutherford and Barbara Weitbrecht.

Thanks to Kathleen Cantwell for her superb cover design.

Special thanks and love to my wife Lee T. Budahn, who makes all things possible.

The song sung by the tour group from Ohio, "Why Oh, Why Oh," is from *Wonderful Town*, copyright 1953, lyrics by Betty Comden and Adolph Green, music by Leonard Bernstein.

Check our website at SpectersAnonymous.Com.

Made in the USA
Middletown, DE
20 April 2019